IMPERFECTIONS

By

Tatum Tricarico

Imperfections

ISBN-13: 978-1-69948-818-8

Contents

For the people who feel broken
to know that the work of God will be displayed through them.

John 9:1-5

Chapter One

Inside the Room

"Will! He here! Up! Up! He Here!"

Will heard the clinking of the opening door, the enthusiastic instructions of his friend, and the moans and yells of those around him before he even opened his eyes for the day. For a moment they made him uncomfortable, as they did every morning, but he told himself not to think anything of it, because he knew that's what happened every day. Somehow the noises still irked him even after all these years. Their consistent, disordered exclamations were completely expected, but still so deeply concerning. They scared him so intensely upon his arrival, but now they held an even more eerie weight. He knew the noises now. He knew the voices. He knew the screams. And he knew, oh so fully, why they were screaming.

That was what made him so uncomfortable now, but he tried his best to ignore the insistent cries and move on with the day. It was all he could do to keep any sort of normalcy.

"Thank you, Jaden. I'm up," Will said, opening his eyes and rubbing them to adjust to the harsh lighting of the fluorescent beams above. He looked over to Jaden and gave him a smile. Jaden smiled back. The two men were similar in age, but Will had a lighter complexion than Jaden.

"You ready, Will? You ready for it?" Jaden said with an excitement that motivated Will. He looked so eager, as if this didn't happen the same way every day. As if for some reason today would be any different. Which, oddly enough, gave Will the fervent hope that maybe it would be. Maybe today would be the day they were listened to. Maybe today would be the day they were heard. Finally.

Both of the young men watched as an older gentleman walked through the heavy door into the room. Will noticed the wrinkles and creases in the man's uniform and he could tell that it had clearly been thrown on in a hurry that morning. Only, Will supposed, that it wasn't really morning for the man. Just for him. The man closed the door behind him with a loud slam, reminding Will once again that he belonged only on the inside.

"Excuse me, Servant," Will said loudly, and with enough urgency that it would have made anyone notice. Anyone except this man, or rather anyone except someone in this man's position.

Will continued nevertheless, with the same desperation as before, "Servant, please. What day is it? What is the date? I would really like to know, Servant, if you would please tell me."

Again, nothing. Always, nothing.

"Is Servant Deena still in power? Do they still watch her, Servant? Or is someone else on the screen now?"

Will looked to Jaden, and seeing the tearful look in his eyes said, "It's okay Jaden. We'll get it tomorrow."

"'Kay, Will," Jaden said bringing back just a glimmer of the hope they had had only moments ago. Will knew, though, that he had lied. He knew they wouldn't get it tomorrow. It would happen again tomorrow just as it did every day.

They sat and watched in dejected silence as the man made his way to each chair in the room. He rolled his cart habitually, clicking and popping the cartons out of the cart and into the backs of each of the big metal chairs. That cart was huge and towered over the man's head, barely fitting through the door because it was holding so many boxes.

One carton would come out of the cart and he would switch it for one that was in the chair that had been used from the day before. He came around quickly as if he wanted to be anywhere but in this room. Will didn't blame him. The smell of decay and the screams and groans of those surrounding him were something that it took years to get used to, and this man clearly didn't want to try. He came in and out every day to switch the food and toilet boxes on the backs of the chairs and then he left as hastily as he entered, probably cursing the fact that this was where he was assigned to work.

He came up to Will's chair. Will turned his head to watch the man pop out the food and toilet packs from behind him. The man was intentional to not make eye contact and more than cautious to never get close enough to be touched by those in the room. Will had tried to reach for him once, to try to get him to listen, but for days after that the man came nowhere near Will and refused to replenish his food or toilet box. Will was careful never to try that again and eventually the man dropped the issue and continued to serve Will in the way that he served the others.

Will tried one last time, hoping Jaden wouldn't hear. "Servant, I promise you, I understand. Just please tell me, what is happening. What is the date? Where is Grace Josephs? Is she still alive?"

Nothing.

There were some days that Will wanted nothing more than to hear that his mom was still out there. Then he could believe the things she told him when he was eight, the last time he had seen her. But he knew this man wouldn't give him an answer and he tried not to wonder why he asked. Hope was the only thing that held him together, and the more he wondered, the more he thought about the pointlessness of it all, and the quicker his hope depleted. So instead he decided to not think at all. He had gotten good at that by this point.

The man left quickly after changing all of the boxes in the chairs.

Jaden turned to Will. "It's time, Will. Yes?"

"Almost," Will said this time matching his enthusiasm.

For years, there was absolutely nothing that brought Will joy in here. From the time he was brought in as an eight-year-old, until, he was guessing, the age of twelve. But at age twelve, he could finally remember again the words his mother said to him on the last day of his life outside, and he realized he needed to do something.

That's when he started training.

The large metal chairs that each of them were locked in had straps around the middle of the waist and around each leg. He realized then that the Servants had made a huge oversight with him, and he was thankful that no one had noticed. One of the reasons that Will had been put in the room was that after the accident they had to amputate both of his legs above the knee. The residual limbs he had now were only about a few inches on each side. Because of that, neither of the leg straps on the chairs were able to lock him in. That meant that at night, when the chairs lowered down and turned to beds, Will could jerk himself out of the single strap around his waist and get out of the chair, completely. Once he realized this, he started working on his arm strength enough to lift himself up and down from the chair while it was reclined and move around on what was left of his legs.

Now he slept during the "day" when the chair was upright and he was confined, but as soon as it went down, he would slip himself out. Today, he heard the chairs chirp, as they do every day, in their high-pitched, condescending tone, "Nighty Night. Let's go to bed!" Even now, hearing them speak still gave him the chills. Then all the chairs started leaning backwards together until everyone was lying flat. Finally, they said, "Lights out!" and the room went dark.

That's when Will slipped out.

Years ago, he spent his time out of the chair working to try to unlock the door. But after what he counted out as a year and a half, he finally understood that because of the intricacies of the locks, opening the door was not something he would ever be able to do. At the same time, he also knew that he needed something to focus on or he would go crazy. By that point, the noises of the cries of the others and the chairs' voices trying ineffectively to console them were no longer scary, and the smell of decay and rotting were no longer something he noticed at all. They were just his every day. They were just his normal. But he knew that they shouldn't be. And that's when he started to wonder about the others. Did this have to be their normal, or did they too deserve something more?

That's when Jaden came. Jaden and his almond-shaped eyes. Jaden and his slurred words. Jaden and his tongue that sticks out just a bit farther than normal. But most importantly, Jaden with *words*. None of the others in the room with Will could speak, or at least they couldn't speak enough to have a conversation. Mostly this was because, Will later assumed, they were taken from their parents and "raised" by their baby-voice, fake-consoling chairs, because that's what the Servants believed was best for them. But Jaden, he could talk. Will soon learned that this was because his mother was able to keep him hidden from the Servants for long enough to teach him. Will then started working with him to improve his speech skills little by little every day, until finally he had someone who he could talk to, and that was when this place became a lot less lonely.

Together, Jaden and Will noticed that they were not the only two who might be more capable than the Servants thought when putting them in here. Will remembered what his mother's last words to him were, and realized that they applied not only to him, but to all the others in this room as well. Certainly to Jaden, but really to all the others, though in different ways. They were better than this room. They weren't broken. They were created in God's image too, regardless of what the Servants thought. Once Will realized this, things started to change.

Now, at age 26, he started his daily, or rather nightly routine that he had already done a thousand times and still, he knew would probably do a thousand more. But he also knew that one day things might be different, so he did this in case that day ever came. He hoped it would. Jaden hoped it would. The others probably hoped it would too, in their own way.

Will pulled himself out of his chair as it whispered, "Shhhh. It's okay. You're okay. Shhhhh," assuming that his movement was due to discomfort. The Servants programmed them to parrot that sentiment every time one of them cried or yelled or moved too much. This, among other things, bothered Will the most because he knew that he and the others deserved more than that. The Servants of course said it was good for them. They said that it was helpful and what they needed, but Will knew it wasn't. He knew they needed love and friendship and connection, so he would do his best to give that to them tonight, as he had every night before.

He lowered himself out of the chair and started his rounds the same way he had every night for years. He moved to a small, quiet girl in the chair closest to him on the left. "I'm right here, friend. I'm right here," Will said softly, but respecting the mental capability he knew she had while still knowing that she could not see him. When he first went to her years ago, she was scared, for he assumed she had been here since her parents found her blind at birth. Now, as Will approached her, she stopped her nervous, repetitive rocking and relaxed.

Will reached out and held her hand gently. He imagined that she was probably nine or ten years old now, one of the youngest in the room. Because of that, she was probably the most accustomed to his touch. He had been making his rounds most of her life. As she wrapped her hand around his, he sat down on the edge of her chair, which was laid out as a bed just like the rest of them were. He knew that if she grew up without physical touch, as many of the others had, then she would be not only more unhappy, but also more disconnected and less well-adjusted. Because of this, he used his time with her and all the others every day to hold their hands. As he did this more and more, he found their screams to be less frequent and intense.

As he sat next to her, holding her hand between both of his, he said to her what his mom said to him so many years ago. "Child," he said, "I love you. And God loves you. You were sent to this place because the Servants thought that you could not handle the real world. They thought you were too broken, too imperfect, to be with them and that this room would help you. But they were wrong. Friend," he continued, "You are not helpless, you are not broken. The God that we follow does not make mistakes. You are perfect, just as perfect as all of the Servants, just as perfect as anyone else. You are strong, you are loved, and you are capable. You do not belong in this place. You belong in the Sovereignty. Never forget that. You can be independent. You can be powerful. You are. So, use that power to one day let the Sovereignty know that you are worthy. Get out. You can do it. You were made to show the Sovereignty what they were missing. Don't live your whole life in here. Get yourself out. Show them that you are worthy. Because you *are* worthy."

Will added the last sentence his mother said the last time they had talked, but over the years he realized that it was better phrased a bit differently. "Friend, they will see us again."

Will's mind went back to the first time he had heard these words. He pictured his mom leaning over him in his hospital bed. She of course had referred to it as "that place" rather than "this place" and spoke in terms of the future. But still Will knew it was words they needed to hear during their time here, however long that might be. He thanked God each time he said these words, for they were the only thing that got him and the others through their day. He specifically thanked God for the fact that he remembered them, because after the accident, his memory had left him for a few years. When he was twelve, these words came back to him as did much of his memory of the Sovereignty outside. That's when things began to change in him, and he hoped that by repeating these words to the others that he would be able to bring some of that change to their lives too.

This girl whom he was whispering them to now was very intelligent. Will assumed that the only reason she had been placed in here was due to her blindness. He knew this, because she whispered back to him after he finished. She repeated word for word, flawlessly what he said. Finishing too with, "Friend, they will see us again," but what she didn't understand was that she could use these words, too. Will wished he could show her the world and show her that everything had a name and a word. He wanted to show her that she had the power to use the words and change his sentences up, but because she was locked in the chair, she could not feel the things around her nearly well enough to understand that concept. For now, Will spoke other things to her, too. He tried every day to have her repeat every word he could think of in hopes that she would learn how to form them with her mouth, which she did easily. Then one day, hopefully she would get to connect those words to real things. He said things like tree, house, dog, television, hope, joy, and love. Maybe if he whispered them and she repeated them enough, one day she would get to know their meanings and experience them. But for now, she would just say what he said, and that would have to be enough because he could not show her more no matter how badly he wished he could.

He whispered one last time the words "I love you" to her as he lowered himself off of her chair, let go of her hand, and staggered over to the next one. This man was much older and had clearly been here since long before Will arrived. Will supposed that he had been here since birth, as most of them were, because he did not like being touched. The first time Will had attempted to reach out to this man was the only time he had been hurt by one of the others. The man was fairly quiet during the day, but if he was touched he would let out screams as if he were in pain. Will knew it was still important that this man have some sort of physical contact so that he would be comfortable with people if he were ever to get out.

After years of working with him, Will had gotten him to a point where the man was no longer upset by being touched on his feet. Anywhere else, and the man would lash out, but now daily Will could come and stroke his feet without screaming or kicking or anger. The man actually seemed to quite enjoy it now, but still would not allow Will to move past his ankles, let alone try to hold his hand. Will continued to do this every day hoping that eventually the man would become more accustomed to human touch. He also knew that this was a man who did not handle even tiny changes in lighting or placement of his chair well, so changing how he felt about physical touch would be a long process. Will was willing to try, though.

Once he had spent a bit of time rubbing his feet, he moved up to near his head. Will locked eyes with him and tried to hold eye contact for as long as he could, knowing that the man was uncomfortable with that, too. As their eyes met for a brief second, Will started whispering the words that he knew so well by heart. The words of his mother to him. The words of him to all the others. As he said them, he bent in as close as he could to the man without leaning near enough to be hit by his arms. He told this man these words as he did every day, hoping that they would sink in. Hoping that somehow this man would grow enough to know these things at least in his heart and to fully feel loved, because in here, that's all that they had.

After he whispered his mother's words, he went back and rubbed the man's feet once more. After a few more minutes, he moved onto the next chair. He spent the next number of hours making his rounds to these chairs and speaking love and life over the others in ways that he could only hope would make a difference. Just to know that he was doing something to make his mom's affirmations heard in their lives and in his life as well was something that warmed his heart and quite literally kept him alive in this isolated room.

Will knew that there were one hundred and eight others in this room, and sometimes this made his rounds overwhelming, but today it gave him a sense of power and connectedness as it did most of the time. For years he felt so lonely, but now by reaching out to the others every day, he knew he was needed and knew he was loved. He might not be seen as "perfect" by those outside of this room, but he knew that God was using him within it.

Hours later, Will had made it through almost all of the others, and only had his two last chairs to visit. These two chairs were special because they were the only two of the others that he saved. For all the others, he would just visit in a circle making his way around the room, but these two were important for Will to come back to last.

The first one was a young girl, probably in her late teens. Will could tell that she was absolutely brilliant. Though he knew that she was unable to speak, he saw her mind going a hundred different directions all at the same time. He could tell at least that in some sense, she could understand the words that he whispered over her each night, though she could not verbally respond. He could not yet whisper those things to her today, though, because they had to do their daily ritual first. Their ritual started about six years ago, almost a month after she was brought in. Because this girl was so incredibly intelligent, she was able to work mechanics in ways that Will knew he never could. He thought of all the things that her skill could be used for, that would be so very helpful in the real world, but in this room, that skill just caused her pain.

The problem was that she was so good at understanding machines and mechanisms that she was able to unlock the chains around her legs and waist. For the first few days that she was in this room, Will would watch her spend hours fiddling with the locks until she finally was able to get them to click off. She then would jump out of her chair and run to the door. Again a few hours would go by and then suddenly Will would hear the heavy metal door unlock and open. She would walk through it just as Will wished he could. Within a matter of moments though, the man from the outside who came in each day would grab her and drag her back in by her feet so he would not have to be near her face or hands in case he were to get hurt. He would violently toss her back into her chair and lock the chains around her legs and waist yet again. Then, just as quickly as he had come in, he would leave, slamming the huge door closed and locked behind him. The girl would start right back into trying to get the chains off, and by about the same time the next day, the same thing would happen again.

At first, Will thought about one day following behind her out the big door. He knew though that his walking was all but quick and definitely not graceful enough to avoid the man trying to drag him back in. No matter what, even if he did try, he knew that getting out for a moment and then being forced back in would not help him, nor would it help anyone in here get any closer to freedom. Will watched this girl with amazement though seeing her dedication to her goal give her a drive to constantly fight the chains holding her. He knew that this would be a good thing if she could just be accepted by the Servants in the Sovereignty. But for now, it served as inspiration for him to continue so passionately in his goal of helping the others see their worth and feel that they are loved.

About a month after she arrived, the guard apparently got tired of chasing after her every day, and so he did something that Will could never erase from his memory. One day, after the man dragged her back in and locked her back up and left the room, he returned again with a large aluminum baseball bat. Will was scared of what he was planning to do and watched him go directly over to the girl, swing the bat, and hit her hard on the legs. It seemed that he had either disconnected them from their socket at the hip or just broken them altogether. Her screams still rang in his ears. She was a very quiet girl, but that day she spent most of her time screaming. It hurt Will almost physically to hear her painful cries. He tried to help, but he couldn't do much to fix her pain.

Even through the hurt though, her obsession continued, and she worked to unlock herself from her chair yet again. The first time she did this after having her legs broken, she attempted to stand up and run out of her chair, but just fell flat on the floor. She cried out loudly in pain again. Will ran over and worked to lift her up and sit her back in her chair. He assumed that this was what the man hoped would happen. That she would never be able to walk out of the room again, even if she unlocked herself from the chair.

On that first day, it was quite a challenge for Will to get her back up in her chair, but she still had the constant obsession to unlock the binds attaching her to her chair. Will was thankful that it took her a few hours to get them completely unlocked, so she only managed to do it about once a day. Sadly, because her legs never healed correctly, she still repeated this pattern of unlocking the chains and falling to the floor every day. Getting the timing right took a few days, but Will found out that he was the only one who would ever put this girl back up to get food and use the toilet on her chair. If he left her, the man would come in, load the food and toilet pods in her chair and leave her lying on the floor. Occasionally if this happened, the man would even give her a little kick or shove out of the way, which would lead to screaming, which was washed over by all the other yells in the room, but Will still heard. He finally got a system together where he would reach her at the end of his rounds and put her in her chair so that she would not miss any of the food the chair gave her, and would be in the seat when the man came back in so that he could not hurt her anymore.

Now, after almost five years of picking her up and lying her back in her chair, Will and the girl had a rhythm down that worked for both of them. It no longer caused her pain or was an issue for Will to manage. He quickly set her back in her seat and sat down next to her. He held her hand and whispered the words of his mother to her, stressing them more deeply because he knew she understood their meaning on some level more than just the tone of his voice. The words "Because you are worthy," echoed in the space between them and hung for a moment. Then he pulled her into a tight embrace and said, "Friend. They will see us again."

He let go of her her, locked her waist and feet to the back of the chair and went over to Jaden. He always finished his rounds with Jaden so that he could work with him on speech. He sat down next to him, took his hand, and whispered the words for the last time that day, and Jaden whispered back. "'Cause you worthy, Friend, they see us 'gin."

"Thank you Jaden," said Will still lying with him.

"You welcome, Will, you welcome!" he replied with his constant enthusiasm.

"I love you, Jaden."

"Love you too, Will. Love you too," then he continued, "Time to go, Will. Breakfast time."

"You're right Jaden," Will said pulling himself down from Jaden's chair. It was time for breakfast so he had to make it back to his chair before it went back up to a sitting position, or he couldn't get back in. His chair and Jaden's were about four away from each other, which was something Will was thankful for every day. Being able to have conversations with him was something, if not one of the only things, that kept Will sane in the room. But it was time to go now, so he left Jaden and quickly hobbled back to his chair, hoisted himself up, and squished back into the strap that now rested around his waist.

Within minutes, the chairs echoed in unison, "Wake up, sweetheart, wakey wakey," and slowly raised their backs so that Will and all of the others were in a sitting position. Again, a few minutes passed, with more screaming than usual due to the sudden change that only happened twice a day. After about five minutes, the chairs all spoke again, saying, "Time for food. Here's your breakfast!" Will cringed at how condescending it all was. He thought that eventually it would stop bothering him, but instead, now it just bothered him more, knowing that it was affecting all the others just as much as him.

The arm of the chair reached out directly in front of his face with a little pod of food about the size of a biscuit. It moved towards his face until Will opened his mouth and ate it. It was just the same as it was every day, probably because it was the easiest way to get the right amount of nutrition to him and all the others, but the never changing dryness and denseness of his food patty was one of the hardest things for him to accept in this room. He was sure that the Servants thought they were doing the right thing, by providing him and the others with this "food" that would be enough to keep them alive, just as they thought the chairs' voices were helping comfort them in the room. But Will knew what was really happening. They just wanted to say that they were "serving" the "least of these" as their God had called them to do. Only, Will knew they weren't. Will knew they were just trying to reach their own level of likeness to God, and he and the others were just the casualties of their race to perfection.

He let it go for now though, opening his mouth and eating his food patty, and waiting for the chair to say "Drink your water. Here it comes." He quickly drank the water being poured in his mouth, and then leaned back into the chair. It was time to sleep now, so that he could wake up yet again and do the same thing tomorrow. He thought through his day and remembered his mother's words one last time, reciting them to himself before he closed his eyes and got to leave the room, if only in his mind, for a few hours, as he slept.

The words from his mother echoed in his dreams that night, "Because you are worthy, William Isaac Josephs, and I will see you again."

Chapter Two

New Hope

"Will! He here! Up! Up! He Here!"

Will opened his eyes for another day. "Thanks Jaden, and good morning!" He leaned as far forward and as far backward as he could trying to stretch his back from his short night's sleep sitting up in his chair. He quickly paused though, because all of a sudden the atmosphere in the room changed.

Will and the others heard the locks click on the giant door separating them from the Sovereignty, just as they did every day, but as soon as the door swung open, the sounds of screams and moans and babbling increased to a volume even Will wasn't expecting.

Every day for a few minutes when the man walked in, all of the others started crying out a bit louder, for many of them struggled with even the slightest change. This however, was definitely not simply that. They got so much louder, so suddenly, that Will knew something was off. He lifted a short prayer, or rather hope, that it wasn't something bad.

At first, Will didn't notice anything out of the ordinary. The man walked through the door as quickly and apathetically as usual and started coming towards the first chair along the wall. But then Will noticed the difference: Someone was following him.

Will remembered years ago there was a different person who came in. She was just as mean as this man, if not even more. She spent a day training the man that came in now. Since that day, he has been the only one in and out for at least ten years. Those were the only two people who had ever come into the room for the entire time Will had been there. But today was someone new. Today he saw only the third person from the Sovereignty he had ever seen since being outside.

Will knew he still needed to try to get his questions answered, but he was so startled by the extra noise and extra person that he forgot for a moment. He surveyed the scene. They were now clearly in view, no longer blocked by the door. Will could see the person following was a woman with dark hair up in a messy bun. The contrast between her and the man was interesting. The man was so stiff and so hurried with a feeling of disregard. She, on the other hand, seemed to have something kinder about her, or at least something more energetic.

"Okay, now Servant... Samantha, right?" as the man spoke, the yells from the others increased.

"Samantha Keener," the woman replied. Her voice was high and with a tune of joy that Will had not heard from anyone, except maybe Jaden, for years.

"Servant Samantha..."

"No, please just call me Samantha."

"Well, um, Samantha, can you grab that cart and roll it over here for me?"

Will had never heard anyone ask to not be called a Servant. Servant Deena, the woman in charge of their Sovereignty, had been in that position for many years, and many people were there before her. They all intentionally were called Servant and every person in the workforce wanted that title, too. Will didn't know where it started, but he knew that he wished he could be called a Servant. The Holy Book told them that to be more like God they had to serve each other, and so, in order to strive for the perfection that God is, everyone in the society adopted the title of Servant. Will knew many years ago, there were different titles for men and women, but that was no longer necessary for they were all viewed the same now. Everyone was made in God's image. Therefore, everyone had to strive to meet the image of God: perfection. By being called Servant, they believed they could do this.

But Will would never be called a servant. None of the others here would either, because no one believed they were created in the image of God, because they had something wrong so they couldn't be *perfect*. They would never be called servants because they could never even attempt to reach the level of perfection that a servant had achieved. But they could be served. And that's what the servants believed they were doing by sending this man in once a day and by having the chairs say cute things to them. That wasn't serving really though, and Will knew that. He wondered if maybe this woman knew that, too. It was so curious that she would deny her title of servant. It was denying her attempt at perfection and Godliness. Why she would ever do that? It seemed foolish. He would definitely be called a servant if he could be.

"Here you go," Samantha said. There was a kindness in her voice that Will hadn't heard in ages. It was soothing, like music or medicine.

"Take out the two boxes on the top right corner."

"Okay."

"Now take these used boxes out of the back of the chair. Careful that one doesn't spill."

"Got it."

"Now switch 'em. That's all you've got to do."

Samantha put the empty food box and the full toilet box back in their place in the huge cart. She stopped though before putting the next one in.

"That's it?" she asked struck with the simplicity of the job.

"Yep. They faster you do that, the faster you can get out of here," the man said, clearly not noticing the troubled look on her face.

"Oh. Okay. How long does it normally take you?"

The man smirked. "I can get out of here in an hour if I do it right."

"Wow. You can get through one hundred and eight people that fast?"

"They're not people, Servant Samantha. They're creatures. People were created in the perfect image of God. These creatures are not perfect, not human."

"Yes," Samantha said quickly, looking engaged in what he was saying and wiping the agitated look off her face. "You're right, you're right. Creatures."

But Will noticed the way she said creatures didn't come out naturally, or pleasantly. She didn't want to say it. He wished she wouldn't. Even though he didn't know this woman at all, somehow it hurt him to hear her call him a creature even more than it did when the man said it. He had higher expectations for her, but he should have known not to get his hopes up. He was all he had in here. Himself, and maybe Jaden.

"Now let's get a move on," the man asked, grabbing the next set of boxes. "If you take half and I take half, you'll learn it well enough, and we'll be out of here in half an hour so I can have some time to prepare my outfit for my first day of my new job tomorrow."

"Okay. Can I take this half, though?" Samantha asked pointing to the side with Will, Jaden, and the girl who could unlock her restraints.

"Sure," the man said, already working, "Doesn't matter to me."

Samantha walked over to that side and started switching the boxes of food and feces Will saw that she tried not to meet his eyes or any of the others, but he didn't think it was for the same reason the man didn't. There was something else.

He suddenly remembered that he needed to speak up. "Excuse me, Servant," he said to her.

She turned to look at him.

"What is the date today? And is Servant Deena still in power?"

Samantha took a step towards him, but the man noticed and motioned for her to stop. He waved her away and said, "Don't listen to them,

Servant Samantha. He's just spewing words. It took me a while to believe that too, but the servant who trained me explained it to me. He's just saying things he's heard before. None of it means anything to him. I know it sounds like it does, but it doesn't. He always asks the same questions, he's just repeating something he's heard before."

Will was stunned. He never knew that was why this man didn't respond. He just figured the man didn't care, but that actually made some sense. He had been asking the same questions every day. Suddenly he was angry that he hadn't realized that sooner. Maybe he could have done something more.

Samantha seemed stunned, too. "Are you sure? It sounds like he knows what he's asking about."

"I'm sure. And I can promise you, if you don't believe me and you try to engage with him, or any of the creatures, it won't end well. We are called to be in community with the people and the Sovereignty that God created. These creatures aren't part of that. They're flawed. They're not created in the image of God. We shouldn't go messing around with them. We're being kind enough just taking care of them so well."

Will shuttered. He didn't like listening to this man talk. Something told him that Samantha didn't, either. She looked over at him one more time.

The man's voice was hard and cold, like granite. "Ignore him, Servant."

"It's just Samantha," She said to him quietly, or maybe more to herself, and then once he turned away she met Will's eye. *Sorry.* She mouthed inaudibly. He nodded, understanding, and they both smiled. A tear rolled down his eye and onto his cheek. He wiped it away and closed his eyes. Apart from the others in the room, that was the first time he felt noticed by anyone. It warmed him and it hurt him at the same time.

For a while, Samantha and the man switched the boxes in silence. It was repetitive, but went very quickly. Will wished it would take longer so

Samantha would stay near him, but he also wished she would leave right away. Something felt threatening about the fact that she was building hope in him. It scared him. He knew he shouldn't, but he desperately needed something to put his hope in. Already he was terrified of what would happen if he was forced to lose hope in her. He decided he couldn't think like that anymore. She would be just like the man, and that was all that would happen. That's what he told himself, anyway, and that's what he needed to believe to stay strong.

Suddenly, he heard yelling to his side. He turned quickly to see what the problem was. The man turned, too. Some of the others were screaming louder right around the girl who could unlock her restraints. Will's heart started beating quickly. Did he get her locked in right or had she gotten out while the servants were here? He didn't know what they would do if she had, but it would not be good or pleasant.

It wasn't the others that were doing all of the screaming, though. The man let out a quick scream, too. Will finally saw what was going on. Samantha had gotten close to the front of the girl's chair and the girl had reached out and swiftly grabbed Samantha's arm.

Tears rolled down Samantha's cheeks. The girl would not let go. Screams echoed from the others and the man came running over. Samantha freed her arm from the girl's grip before the man could violently do it for her. She was still crying though. Sobbing.

"You can't do that, Servant!" He barked. "You absolutely cannot go to that side of the chairs when I'm not here. I could have helped you now, but I won't be here after today. Stay behind the chairs on the outside on the square. If you move to the middle, you might get close enough for them to touch you, and they will hurt you. Do you understand?"

"Yes. I'm sorry. That was foolish of me," Samantha whispered, stepping around to the side of the square, still locking eyes with the girl. Will had never seen this girl make eye contact with anyone, but now she was holding her stare directly at Samantha. Samantha's face, wet with tears, looked like the girl had just broken her heart, rather than hurt her in any physical way. Will wondered if she had been hurt at all. The girl didn't seem to be grasping too strongly. The man ignored Samantha's tears and went back to his work. Eventually, Samantha did the same, but she never fully regained her earlier demeanor. She seemed deflated. Selfishly, Will hoped that it didn't impact her connection with him at all.

He watched the two of them finish their rounds and make their way to the door. As they left, the man looked back at it all for a split second, reflecting perhaps on the time he had spent in this room over the years. This gave Samantha time to look over in their direction once more. Will could tell she was trying to meet the eyes of the girl, but the girl was already working to unlock her waist restraint. Samantha smiled at the girl and then looked over at Will. He smiled back at her, and she gave him a distinct wink. He wondered what it meant and he wouldn't stop wondering about its meaning for the rest of the day.

The two servants walked out quickly after that, but their presence left a feeling in the room that Will could not deny. He couldn't get his mind off of the woman's word and her wink. He smiled every time he thought of it.

"Samantha Keener," he said out loud. He liked the sound of it. If he were being completely honest, he just liked the *idea* of it. The idea of knowing someone had noticed him. Repeating her name made that feeling real. Made *him* feel real. She *knew* him. She would remember him on the outside. And she would see him again tomorrow.

"Samantha Keener!" Jaden exclaimed, repeating Will.

"Yep, Jaden. Samantha Keener. Not a servant. Just Samantha. Samantha who looked me in the eye, who winked, and who said sorry. Samantha who touched that girl."

"Samantha," Jaden said. "She coming back tomorrow, Will?"

"Yep Jaden. She is. And I can't wait."

"But not with the man, Will?"

"No Jaden. That man is not coming back."

"Good," Jaden said excitedly, "He not nice."

"No Jaden, he's definitely not nice," Will laughed to himself.

"Samantha nice, Will?"

"Oh Jaden, I sure hope so."

At that, the chairs said, "Nighty Night. Let's go to bed!" and reclined so that the others could fall asleep. Looking around, Will saw everyone forcibly lying on their backs staring up at the ceiling with its bright fluorescent glare. The chairs spoke again in their high-pitched trill, "Lights out!" Will closed his eyes for the swift change in light and opened them again to complete darkness. He started wiggling himself out of the binds around him and shifted down to the floor. He shimmied over to the girl closest to him who was blind. He started his rounds with her every day, but today he was barely present. He couldn't get the events of the day off of his mind.

He whispered his mother's words to the girl. "Child, I love you. And God loves you. You were sent to this place because the Servants thought that you could not handle the real world. They thought you were too broken, too imperfect, to be with them and that this room would help you. But they were wrong. Friend, you are not helpless, you are not broken. The God that we follow does not make mistakes. You are perfect, just as perfect as all of the Servants, just as perfect as anyone else. You are strong, you are loved, and you are capable. You do not belong in this place. You belong in the Sovereignty. Never forget that. You can be independent. You can be powerful. You are. So, use that power to one day let the Sovereignty know that you are worthy. Get out. You can do it. You were made to show the Sovereignty what they were missing. Don't live your whole life in here. Get yourself out. Show them that you are worthy. Because you are worthy. Friend, they will see us again."

He didn't think about these words as he said them this time in the way that he usually did. He said them quickly, still with meaning, but hoping that if he moved in a hurry somehow time would pass faster, and Samantha would be here sooner. He thought that maybe something would be different with her here. He hoped it would, and though he didn't want to admit it, this was the strongest hope that he had had in the last nineteen years.

As he spoke, he thought of her and all he would say when she arrived. Would he ask the same questions that he did to the man? Or would he try to talk to her like a friend? Because she did not want to be called Servant, Will figured she was different from the rest. But how different? And *why* was she different? And how could Will get her to use that difference to help himself and the others? Or was she just like the rest of them?

These questions swarmed through his mind all day and he could do nothing to make them stop. He knew he shouldn't be so hopeful, but any change could be good change. Or bad change, and he wondered about that, too. But with the way all of the others were still reacting, he was not able to ignore the quite literal transformation in the atmosphere that her presence commanded, even hours after she left. Will noticed it, and all the others did, too.

Finally, Will was coming to the end of his rounds. He reached the girl who had unlocked herself from her restraints and was on the floor yelling. He picked her up as he did every day, but today he pictured her hand wrapped around Samantha's wrist. He pictured Samantha's tears and their eyes locking and how easily Samantha was able to get the girl to let go. Will longed for that physical touch that they had had, even if just for a second.

As he lifted her back into her chair, her hair brushed against his face and she reached up to tuck it behind her ear. Her hand moved swiftly right under Will's nose. He sprang back, startled not by her hand, but by the smell. It must have been her hand, but maybe even her hair, that smelled like Samantha. Will didn't think it could be real, though. He must have just been making it up. He couldn't have smelled her earlier today. They weren't close enough, he thought. But maybe they were, because this girl smelled the same. Will figured he was crazy, or if nothing else, that the girl's hand smelled like Samantha just because they had touched. This was one of the moments, though, where Will knew that the intensity and terror of being confined to this room had taken a toll on him. He never would have imagined that they smelled the same, or even if he were correct, he never would have noticed their smell at all if his life had been normal. If he hadn't been confined by the Servants to this absurd lifestyle.

He quickly finished his time with the girl, making sure to strap her in tightly as he left, so that she would make it to the end of the next day in her restraints and not fall out before he could get back to her. He always felt bad doing this, but he felt worse when she was left lying on the ground crying out and he couldn't do anything about it, and far worse the few times she had gotten out while the man was there, and he pushed her off to the side with his feet. That made Will sick.

Hustling over to Jaden, Will tried to get the smell out of his mind. He tried to get Samantha out of his mind. But it was no use. He spent time with Jaden working on Jaden's talking, holding his hand, and repeating Will's mother's words to each other. "Friend, they will see us again," Will whispered. But he thought of Samantha. She had seen him. She had mouthed the word "sorry" clear as day. She communicated with him. She saw him. He wondered if she had given him a second thought once she left the room. He hoped she had. The feeling of being seen and heard was what compelled him to think of her, he realized. Just in interacting with him, she had made him know he was seen by someone other than Jaden and the others. By someone other than his mom. By someone on the *outside*. That feeling wrapped around his heart and mind and didn't leave room for much else.

Jaden whispered, "Friend, they will see us again," and Will thought of the millions of people outside these walls. They would see him again, wouldn't they? Or would he stay unseen and unwanted for the rest of his life. His thoughts were too much for him right then.

"I have to go back now, Jaden," He said getting up.

"It not time yet, Will." Jaden said sadly.

"I know Jaden, but I went faster today, and now I need some sleep." If he could just sleep, then morning would come and he would get his questions answered. Then he could stop hoping she would see him again and know if she would or if it would all go back to normal. Either way, Will wanted to know.

"'Kay Will. Go back now. Go to bed, Will," Jaden smiled.

"Thanks Jaden."

"You 'kay, Will? You 'kay?"

"Yeah, Jaden. I'll be fine."

"'Kay, Will. Night!"

"Goodnight, Jaden!" Will said, giving him a kiss on the forehead and returning to his chair.

"Love you, Will."

"Love you, too, Jaden. Love you, too."

Will laid back down in his chair and attempted to clear his thoughts and fall asleep.

Chapter Three

Unrestrained

"Will! SHE here! Up! Up! SHE HERE!"

Will's eyes shot open. He had barely closed them at all that night. Nothing could slow his mind down after what had happened yesterday. With nothing changing at all for nineteen years, this felt monumental, and he was sure it did for the others too, even if they didn't know what it meant. Honestly, he didn't know what it would mean either, but that didn't stop him from guessing.

"Oh Jaden. I hope today is good," Will said, inhaling deeply, hoping he was ready for whatever the day held, whether that was a new friend, or nothing at all.

"Me, too, Will. Jaden, too!" The excitement in Jaden's voice warmed Will's heart and made him smile.

They both watched as the door eased open. Samantha emerged, pulling the cart behind her. For some reason, this image made Will nervous. What if she really was just like the two people before her? What if she didn't see him? What if she looked right past him, just as they did?

She awkwardly wheeled the giant cart in and closed the door. She was looking straight ahead at the wall, not making eye contact or acknowledging Will or any of the others closer to her.

"Samantha," Will whispered to himself. "Samantha Keener." Somehow saying her name made him feel better. The only name he had known for nineteen years was Jaden, and that was only because Jaden's father and mother had taught him how to say it before he got taken away. Having even just another name to know was special to him. It gave him hope of one day having people learn his name, too. People like Samantha Keener. But that seemed so far away.

But he figured this was his shot, so he tried to call out to her.

"Suh... Samantha?" His voice wavered.

She jumped and he waited, but she didn't turn. Her eyes stayed fixed on the wall and she continued switching out the boxes in the chairs around her.

"Samantha?" Will said stronger.

Then suddenly, without turning to look at him she replied harshly, "Not now."

Will's heart dropped, and his shoulders fell. Her reaction hit him deeper than he thought it would. Had she just said nothing, it would have been like any other day. Had she entered into the conversation he hoped they would have, he would have been ecstatic. To know that she heard him and pushed him to the side hurt more than anything he had expected. He sat quietly, waiting for something else, but nothing came.

What could she have meant by "not now"? At first Will figured she was just angry about being assigned this new job and didn't want to think about it. He wondered though, only holding on to a glimmer of hope, if she really meant "not now." Because "not now" doesn't mean "not ever."

Samantha made her way around the square room clicking the boxes in and out of the backs of the chairs, looking over the heads of all of the others directly at the wall behind them. Will noticed though, that when she got to the girl who could unlock her chains, she skipped her chair. That scared Will, because if the events of yesterday had really bothered her that badly, she may be starving the girl out. That would be terrible. But it had been done before, both to Will and to the girl. He wasn't sure what to think, but his stomach jolted when Samantha skipped her.

After a few minutes, she reached Will's chair. He tried to meet her eye, but she avoided it in every way she could. Will considered speaking again, but if she really meant "not now," then Will didn't want it to turn into "not ever." She moved straight onto the next chair without acknowledging Will or switching his boxes at all. His heart was beating so quickly at this point that he could feel it in his chest and neck. Was he being starved out too? For what? Talking to her?

Suddenly, she turned around, after finishing all of the other chairs in the room. She made a B-line straight to Will and switched his boxes, still not looking him in the eye.

"Thank you," Will whispered without thinking.

"It's nothing," Samantha muttered nodding her head slowly, but still facing the wall, "really. It's nothing."

He didn't reply. He was scared to. But he smiled, knowing she couldn't see. Knowing she knew he was speaking to her was enough for now, and getting a response, even if it wasn't said directly to him, gave him more than enough hope.

Leaving Will's chair, Samantha quickly made her way over to the girl whom she had previously ignored. She pulled the boxes out of her chair and popped the new ones in faster than she had any of the others. Then she did something that Will didn't expect. She didn't head straight for the door, but instead, she sat, or more fell, down against the wall behind the girl and buried her head in her hands. Will could hear sobs. Not tears, but loud, full body sobs. He wanted to ask what was wrong, but he couldn't decide if it was the right thing to do.

Samantha sat there for minutes sobbing and Will started crying too, although he was not sure why. Her sadness hurt him. She looked so broken. Will wished he knew why she was crying. He just wanted to go over and comfort her, but with his chair upright, he couldn't get out.

Her tears subsided, and she looked up, leaning her head against the wall. The bun on the top of her head hit the wall and smushed forward and she slunk down and looked to the ceiling, shaking her head ever so slightly.

Will could barely make out a slight whisper. "I'm here now, though. I'm here now. I made it."

What? Will definitely didn't see that coming and couldn't understand why she was crying. No one wanted to be here. For the most part, Servant Deena just assigned people to their jobs, but this one was different. A servant had to work in this room for years before they could work directly with Servant Deena. It was a screening process to see if the servant who was trying to work for Servant Deena had enough devotion to her and to the Sovereignty to be loyal and move up the ranks. The only people who did this job were ones who were trying to get promoted to something better. Will couldn't figure out why Samantha would say "I made it." This wasn't the place you made it to. This was just an unwanted stepping stone.

Will watched intently as Samantha picked herself up off the floor and stood behind the girl's chair. She slowly walked forward and bent down in front of it. The girl met Samantha's gaze. Samantha cried.

"I made it, Love. I told you I would. I'm so sorry it took so long," Samantha mumbled through tears.

Will didn't understand.

He waited, deeply curious.

Samantha moved toward the girl in the chair. She sat all the way down on the floor and laid her head down on the girl's lap. The girl reached out and grabbed her bun, holding it for a second and then moving her hand down to stroke Samantha's face. Her hand rested on her cheek.

"Oh Victoria," Samantha whispered, "I love you so much. You're so strong. You're so special. I promise I won't let you go again, Love. I promise."

Will barely noticed the tears falling down his face, too. Even though he still didn't fully know why Samantha was crying, his heart was hurting for her. He figured he shouldn't interrupt yet, though.

Samantha moved her head off of Victoria's lap and looked her up and down, "I wish I knew what's been happening to you, Love. I wish I could hear what's been going on for you all these years. I'm sorry I didn't know, Love. You know I wish I did. I got here as fast as I could."

Victoria gave her a knowing look and then dropped eye contact again. Samantha kept looking at her, though.

"I know what happened to her, Samantha," Will said quietly. She turned her head to fix her gaze on him for a second. He continued, "I've been here the whole time."

Will forgot that he wanted Samantha to notice him. There was something bigger going on and his hopes had all faded away, only now hoping that Samantha was okay. He wished that he knew what was wrong, and he hoped that he could help her.

"You do? You know what happened to Victoria all these years?" Samantha stopped crying and sat there breathing deeply.

"I do know. And I can tell you, but may I ask why you want to know?" Will figured it would impact how he told her story.

Samantha was quiet for a second and looked up at Victoria, smiling deeply. "Victoria's my daughter."

She let those words sink in. Will smiled and they both cried. "I tried to hide her. I tried to keep her with me. But the Servants found her. She could always unlock things so well, I just couldn't keep her contained away from them, she would always break out, and finally they found her and brought her here. I've tried for years to get in here to her, but the only way that I could was by being assigned to this job. To do that, I had to show that I was devoted enough to the Sovereignty to work for Servant Deena. It took years, but I finally convinced them to let me come. Every day I asked. Every day I tried. But I couldn't let them know why I was trying. I had to pretend I was doing it for the Sovereignty. But I was doing it for you, my Love," She turned to Victoria, "I was doing it for you. And I did it. I finally did it." She took Victoria's hand.

"That's why you were crying yesterday," Will understood, "You weren't scared of her. She reached out and grabbed you. She wanted her mom, and you wanted your baby girl. But the man was here so you couldn't connect with her. I thought you were scared. He did, too. But you were crying because you got to touch your daughter again. You weren't scared at all."

"You're right. I just wanted to touch her. I just wanted to sit with her for hours and hold her and know what her life has been like these last six and a half years. I've missed her," Samantha got quieter as she went on and directed her attention to Victoria again, "I've missed you, Love. I've really, really missed you." Will and Samantha could both tell that Victoria understood.

She reached out and grabbed her mom's arm again and looked straight at her as if to say, "It's okay, Mom. I love you, too."

Samantha took a deep breath. "What's your name?" She suddenly asked, looking at Will. Hours ago, all Will wanted was for Samantha to know his name, but instantly it all seemed so trivial. He was just glad she was with her daughter again.

"Will," he said. "I'm Will Josephs." Samantha stood up and walked over to him. She reached out her hand. He took it and they shook hands, looking up at each other for a long time. Will had never been treated like a person in here, let alone treated like an equal, but that's what Samantha was doing right now. It warmed his heart and terrified him at the same time. He didn't feel like he was good enough to be her equal.

"Nice to meet you, Will. I'm Samantha. Samantha Keener."

"Nice to meet you, too, Servant Samantha," Will said, unconsciously trying to tell her that she was better than him--closer to perfect.

"Don't call me that, Will. I don't want to be a servant if it means taking advantage of you and my daughter. That's not serving. That's evil. I don't want to be called that name if those are the people who have caused y'all so much pain in here. I'm nothing special. I'm just like you."

"That's not what the Sovereignty believes," Will countered.

"Well, it's what I believe," Samantha said matter-of-factly, "and it's what y'all need to believe, too. You're just as good as the Servants. Maybe even better because you're not hurting anybody."

Will didn't know what to say. It was hard for him to even think that he could be as good as the Servants after all these years of being ignored and treated like so much less than them. He had stopped viewing himself as equal to them a long time ago and to hear Samantha say it stunned him. The weight of her words hung in the air and seemed to put a physical pressure on his chest, preventing him from responding. Finally, he was able to peek through silent tears.

"Is that why you tried so hard to get here?" he questioned. "Just to make sure your daughter knows that?"

"Partly," she explained. "Of course I want my daughter to feel known and loved and worthy, but I also want all the rest of y'all to know it too. And I knew Del wasn't making that very clear."

"Del?"

"The man who was in here, taking care of y'all all these years."

"More like taking care of our chairs," Will countered. "I didn't even know his name."

"That's why I wanted in so bad. I knew he wasn't doing you justice. I wanted to be here so I could say you were awesome and important, but even more than that, I wanted to get in here to tell the Sovereignty that y'all are awesome and important, because they've got to hear it from somebody."

"They really do," Will said, more to himself than to Samantha.

"It's crazy to me that the Sovereignty still think of y'all as 'less than'," Samantha said shaking her head. "It's not right."

"I don't know," Will admitted. "They seem to think pretty strongly that we just aren't as perfect. There's something wrong with us, and if there's something wrong with us than we couldn't have been made in the image of God." The words had been trapped in him so long, the words just spilled out. All his thoughts and philosophies, held inside for years, burst forth like the breaking of a dam. "There's nothing wrong with God, and there's nothing wrong with the Servants in the Sovereignty. They don't even see us as people like them, because people are made in the image of God. How could we be in the image of God, if there's no potential for us to be perfect like God? And if we aren't in the perfect image of our perfect God, then maybe they're right, maybe we're not people, because people are made in the image of God."

Will had never said this things out loud before. To anyone. He realized that even after all these years of telling himself he was worthy, he had somehow still been overtaken by the idea that he was less than worthy. This came at him through the actions of the two men who had been in the room and the understanding he had about what those in the Sovereignty thought. He had been conditioned to believe he was not enough. He cried harder than he ever had before.

"Will," Samantha stopped his train of thought after a few seconds. "Will, listen to me."

Will looked back up at her, wiping tears from his face.

"There is absolutely nothing wrong with you, Will," Samantha told him, directly looking into his eyes, but possibly too, deep into his heart.

She paused a few seconds, then said it again, "There is nothing wrong with you."

Will looked down at where his legs should be. Samantha's eyes followed his gaze.

"You sure about that?" he asked.

"I am positive."

Will shook his head and laughed to himself.

Samantha stopped him abruptly, "How old were you when you got in here, Will? Did you get very far in school?"

"I was eight, I think," Will took a second to make sure because no one had ever talked to him about that before. "Yeah. I'm pretty positive I was eight when the accident happened, and they put me straight in here because they thought my mind was damaged too. But it wasn't. My memory came back a few years later. I remember a bit of school, but not too much. I was only in the second grade when the accident happened, so just barely getting started. Why do you ask?"

"So you probably don't remember much about the history lessons they taught, do you?" Samantha continued.

"No," Will said, unsure where she was going with this. He thought back to his fleeting memories of his short time in school. He remembered sitting in the front row looking up at his teacher interested to take in his every word. Suddenly he wondered what happened to all of the students who were sitting around him in that memory. He figured they must all be active Servants in the Sovereignty now. They would have already been assigned a job. He wondered where they would have all ended up. Then he had a strange thought. He wondered if any of them had ever thought about where he ended up. He hoped someone in the Sovereignty was thinking about him still.

He remembered his best friend from grade two, Brian, the little boy he sat next to every day. Everything came flooding back. He remembered how much they both enjoyed reading and how whenever he went over to play at Brian's house, Brian's moms would make them snacks and read books to them, sometimes the four of them would read together and sometimes one of Brian's moms would read one book and the other would read another and they would run back and forth and hear all the stories they were telling. They loved learning so much.

Will wondered where Brian and his moms were now. If they ever thought about him, or if he was just a distant memory. These thoughts broke his heart, though, so he went back to the question Samantha had asked.

"I really can't recall much about what I learned in any subject," Will explained. "Is there something I need to remember?"

"Will, do you know what year it is?" Samantha kept going.

"No. What year is it?" Will wished she would just make her point, but he had been trying to get an answer to this question for years, so he figured it might be just as good.

"It's 2298."

Will was surprised. He had been right, "That means I'm 26. I've been here for nineteen years." Somehow, knowing the truth made it feel even longer.

Samantha moved on quickly yet again, so Will's thoughts traveled with her, "If you had been allowed back to school, Will, you would have learned how incredibly ridiculous it is that the Servants think y'all are less than them in this day and age. They should all know so much better by now. It's not like this kind of thing hasn't happened before."

"What do you mean?" Will asked, not sure what she was talking about.

"Have you ever heard of racism?"

"No."

"Have you ever heard of race?"

"No. I'm sorry. I've been stuck in here for so long."

"No, it's not that at all. People don't talk about it anymore."

"Okay," Will said, wondering why she was talking about it now then.

"Race used to be a word to refer to. . .well. . . the color of your skin," Samantha explained.

Will looked down at his arms, "What do you mean, the *color* of my skin?" He looked around at all the others sitting in their chairs and he thought back to his time in the classroom. Did people have a specific *color* of their skin? He thought about it and realized that his skin was a bit lighter than Jaden's. Quite a bit actually. And it was lighter than a few of the others and a few of the people in his memories, too. But it wasn't a different *color*, it was just a different shade.

"People used to see skin as different colors," Samantha interrupted his thoughts, "So like your skin is light and my skin is medium and that person over there has dark skin," She pointed to Jaden, "But years ago, people would say that yours was white, and mine was brown, and his was black."

"That doesn't make sense," Will said adamantly. "It's all just brown, I guess I've known mine is lighter, but I didn't think of it as a different *color.*"

"You're right, Will," Samantha said shaking her head. "We are all just one color on a scale, but people didn't think of it that way a long time ago. People thought that one color skin was good and the other was bad. They believed that God loved people with one color more than God loved people of a different color."

"That's insane," Will said. "They're all still people."

"We know that now," Samantha continued. "But they didn't know that then. People with the 'good' color started telling people of the 'bad' color that their lives were worth less. They started kidnapping them and selling them and forcing them to work and killing them and treating them like animals, or worse."

"Oh my goodness," Will was stunned.

"Finally, though, people started speaking up and saying it wasn't okay. First, it was people with the 'bad' color, and then, it was people with the 'good' color who had heard the people with the 'bad' color, and eventually they stopped selling them as slaves, and bit by bit we got to where we are now."

"The Sovereignty doesn't think that skin is different colors now, do they?" Will asked, puzzled.

"No," Samantha assured him. "It's all one color. Light and medium and dark versions of that color, but all one color, and no one is better or worse because of it, so no one really notices any more at all."

"That's crazy!" Will said, still trying to wrap his mind around it.

"That's what's happening here," Samantha said.

Will stared at her.

"Right?" She asked him.

"I guess." He was still processing it all. "Yeah. Yeah it is. They're telling us we're less than them, but we're not. And they're hurting us and..." he looked around and took in the smells and sights of the decaying people in the room, "and they're killing us. Just because they think we're less than them and because they say that's what God says, too. But I don't think that's what God thinks."

"I don't either, Will," Samantha said, "God is Love, and Love doesn't say y'all are any less than the people on the outside of these walls."

"But the people on the outside of these walls call us creatures," Will reminded her.

"But God calls you Beloved."

Will smiled. No one had called him that before and all he wanted to do was reach up and give her a hug. He couldn't, though, because he was still tied down.

"That wasn't the only time it happened," she said sadly.

"That's crazy."

"It's true, Will. Sadly, it's true. But this time it wasn't about skin."

"What was it about?"

"Gender."

"Gender?"

Samantha nodded. "You're a boy, and I'm a girl. We're different genders."

"Well, I knew that, but why would anyone care?" Will was so confused.

"Years ago, one was looked at as a 'good' gender, and the other was looked at as a 'bad' gender. One was said to be more important and only people of that gender could get jobs and only people of that gender could go to school. It was terrible. People believed that God thought one was worse and the other was better. People even called God one gender and thought that the other gender wasn't in the image of God as much as the 'good' one was."

"That doesn't make sense, either," Will said. "Because gender isn't something that causes something to be better or worse. We're all in the image of God so women and men are just a representation of different parts of God, right? Both genders are in God's image and both genders are people so there isn't a difference of worth."

"We know that now," Samantha said. "But in the past, they truly thought that it made them different enough to be better or worse and they were treated that way. The 'bad' gender got hurt and even killed by the 'bad' gender. People of the 'good' gender used to go around forcing the 'bad' gender to marry them or have sex with them, and then practically owning that person. And sometimes when they owned the person, they would sell them and have other people pay to have sex with them. It was pure evil. Just because everyone saw one gender as 'good' and the other as 'bad'."

"When I was in the Sovereignty," Will recalled, "people said that since we were all people, being a girl or a boy was just a version of that. Kind of like a cat and a dog. They're both house pets and one isn't better than the other, they're just either one or the other. It's different because God made it different so people could have children, not because God chose one over the other."

"You're exactly right, Will," Samantha told him, "It's crazy that they would think that because God made them one way they were better or worse. More or less worthy. God doesn't create people with different worth. He sees everyone as the same level of worthiness."

Will paused suddenly. "But, Samantha, what about the people who aren't 'people'? What about creatures? They aren't created equal. We aren't, are we?"

"Will," Samantha walked closer and put her hand on his shoulder.

"God doesn't call you a creature. That's a word used by the Servants and only the Servants. God calls y'all people. God knows you are just as worthy as any other person, because God made you that way. You are a person. Y'all are. Just like boys and girls are both people and people with different shades of skin are all people. Just because you have something different doesn't mean you're not just as closely in the image of God as every other person in this Sovereignty."

Will took a deep breath in. He was trying so hard to believe what Samantha was saying about him and what she was saying about the world. It was just so hard, because that's not what everyone else thought. Will wanted to believe this so badly that it physically took his breath away. Samantha knew something special. Will wanted that, too. He wanted to know that he was worthy just like the Servants, just as Samantha told him he was. She was right. He knew the truth of it it in his mind, but it was so hard to feel that way when the Sovereignty had hidden him away in this room for so many years. They wouldn't even look at him, and she was saying he was worth just as much as they were. He wished everyone could know what Samantha knew.

"So these other times that people were told they were worthless just because of a difference," Will started. "What did they do? How did they get other people to finally see them as good?"

"They started telling everyone. And then the people they told passed it on to more people. They shared their stories. They made their voice heard. And they got people who didn't have the same differences as them to stand up for them, too."

"So like what you're doing?" Will gave a knowing smile.

Samantha blushed. "Kind of. I mean, I guess. I don't really think of it that way, though."

"But you knew your daughter's story, and now you're passing it on," Will disagreed. "You're being that person."

"I guess," Samantha said. "I just want people to know that y'all are good. I just want them to give y'all the love you deserve. Because this right here," she gestured to the room. "This isn't right."

"No," Will said. "It's not."

"So what are we gonna do about it?" Samantha smiled.

"We?" Will questioned. "How could I do anything? I'm stuck in here."

"They need to hear your story. I heard Victoria's because I got the blessing of living through part of it with her, but the Sovereignty needs to know your story, too. They need to hear all of your stories. Nothing is going to change if they don't understand that your stories are just as important as theirs."

Will thought for a moment, "Well if that's how they stopped thinking differences in skin and gender were bad, then I guess that's what we need to do."

"I'm in!" Samantha smiled.

Will couldn't help but let the excitement build in his stomach. This wasn't just a drop of hope he had had earlier; this was a full ocean, and he was ready to jump right in.

"Me too."

Suddenly they paused. Time had stopped for them both; Will because he was finally seen and Samantha because she finally got to be with her girl. But time had caught back up to them and they didn't realize how long they had been talking. They jumped when they heard each of the chairs cheerfully say, "Nighty Night. Let's go to bed!"

"Oh no!" Samantha said, "I have to get out of here before they say 'lights out' or I'm going to get in trouble with the Sovereignty. They might not let me back in. I have to go." She turned to Will, "I'll see you tomorrow and we'll talk more, Will. We will figure something out to make them see y'all, okay. I promise!"

Will smiled a sad smile. The thought of her leaving hurt his heart. It wasn't a problem that she was going out into the Sovereignty that he wasn't allowed to go in, like it was when the man left. This time it was that she was his friend. His person. And now she would be gone, because regardless if she said it or not, they were believed to have two different "worths," and he had to stay here and she got to leave him, her friend, behind. She had to, and that hurt him so badly he almost cried. But he knew she would feel bad if he did, so he mustered up the courage to quietly reply, "Right. Okay. See you tomorrow."

Samantha turned to Victoria and gave her daughter the biggest hug that she could with her still strapped to the chair. Victoria reached around her and hugged her, too. Samantha cried and Victoria smiled. They stayed there for a second and Will was touched by their bond. He wished that his mother could be in here with him. He knew her words by heart, of course, but somehow getting a hug from his mom right now would make this feeling of loneliness much less painful. He knew that she was somewhere out in the Sovereignty, and he knew, he hoped, he would see her one day, but for now Samantha would have to do. If only they could come up with a plan quickly to change the Sovereignty's mind. It would take a lot, but it was all he wanted in this moment, and he hoped Samantha wanted it even half as badly as he did. He looked up and tried to catch her eye, but she missed his glance.

He watched then as Samantha turned quickly to the door and left.

"Thank you, Samantha," Will whispered so quietly she wouldn't have heard, and then he cried.

"Lights out!"

Chapter Four

The Plan

The hours passed quickly for Will as he made his rounds and then slept restlessly with hundreds of thoughts racing through his head. He replayed everything that Samantha told him, thinking about their implications and their relation to his life in here. Her words echoed in his head right alongside his mother's, reminding him yet again that he was valuable. Those words gave him a new confidence to reach out to all of the others and sit with them and speak the truths of his mother over them. Somehow, her words felt more real after what Samantha had told him, and they seemed more lively coming out of his mouth when he told them to the others. There was hope now. Suddenly, saying, "They will see us again," was no longer a vague idea, but a valid hope with a foundation that might actually take shape into reality. There was excitement now. Will was eager for a plan to develop, and he talked to the others with that newly found passion.

Sleep was a challenge. Normally, that was Will's only way to escape this room, so he usually fell asleep quickly and was swept away in dreaming or just quiet. But today, Will's thoughts were enough of a disruption from the harsh reality that he couldn't clear his mind enough to go into a deep sleep. His thoughts raced, and his heart seemed to beat faster just at the ideas that Samantha had presented to him. Some of it made him excited, some of it filled him with a sense of love, and some of it left him completely confused. Nevertheless, he was intrigued and drawn to her stories and ideas. Will spent a lot of time that morning bouncing ideas off of Jaden and they were both filled with a new joy, which was impressive for the ever-joyful Jaden.

He barely noticed the chairs and their noises today, but he was keenly aware of the others, thinking about their worth too. This idea of Samantha's was not something that was just for him, or just for Victoria. Samantha wanted the value of all of them to be recognized and for them to get to live like they were just as good as everyone else in the Sovereignty. Will thought about what that would look like. It was hard to even picture. Her ideas were just so radical, but also so incredibly simple, that he wasn't sure what it would be like in reality. He hoped that he would be alive long enough to see it play out one day, and that Samantha would have enough drive to actually attempt to change the views of the entire Sovereignty. It was not going to be easy, but Will was sure that Samantha thought it was worth it--that they were worth it.

After hours of conversation with Jaden and Will's failed attempts at sleep, it was time to start the next day. Will was already up when they heard the door start to open and Will and Jaden smiled at each other as Samantha started to walk in.

She shut and locked the door behind her.

"Hi there!" she cheerfully waved to them. "How are y'all doing?"

"'Bout the same," Will said, looking around and laughing a bit.

Samantha smiled, "Guess that's what I figured."

She pulled the cart over and started switching out the boxes in the first chair. Somehow, this made Will uncomfortable. Like by doing this, Samantha was one of 'them'. Obviously, this wasn't true, and she was doing it because it was the only way to get to Victoria and Will and the others, and by doing it, she was keeping them alive, but it still seemed so distant and cold. He chose not to think about it, though. That wasn't going to get him down today. He had so many things he wanted to talk to Samantha about.

"Sam," Jaden said, surprising both Will and Samantha. "You have a plan now? So, they see we good, too?"

He looked up at her, waiting for an answer. Will looked too, just as intently. Samantha laughed, "Wow, you guys are eager, aren't you?"

"You would be, too," Will reminded her.

"You're right, Will," she said seriously. "You are far too right."

"So... you got a plan, Sam?" Jaden asked again.

They all laughed at that, including Jaden. But Samantha just kept switching the boxes as fast as she could.

"Honestly, I really don't," Samantha admitted finally. "But we'll come up with something. I've been thinking about it a lot."

Disappointment set on Will's face for a second, but he saw that Jaden was still optimistic about the fact that she was thinking, so he figured he would be too. It's a start.

"What have you thought about?" Will asked.

"Well, I think that before we can convince the Sovereignty that y'all are awesome, we need to convince yourselves."

That struck a chord with Will, of course, because he had been trying to do that for years, but even yesterday he admitted he didn't believe it himself. It was such a hard balance, but she was right. They had to believe it before they could change anything. Will hoped that some of the stuff he had been saying and doing was helping the others feel like they were valued. He guessed it helped him a little too, but he wasn't sure if it was good enough. He had been trying, but he was honestly a bit embarrassed to tell Samantha, because now that he thought about it, he felt like he could have done something more. He was trying to decide if he was going to tell her or if they would just let her come up with something, but Jaden decided for him.

"Will does that!" Jaden blurted out.

"You do, do you?" Samantha gave him an inquisitive look.

"I mean kind of," Will started to explain. "I just figured, when my memory came back and all, that all the others could use a bit of encouragement, so I've been trying, but I don't know if it's actually done anything."

"I'm sure it has," Samantha assured him. "What have you been doing?"

Will and Jaden spent the next thirty minutes explaining to Samantha all about each of the others and the interactions that Will has with them on a daily basis. He explained which ones were okay with touch and which he could only speak to. They went over the rituals that happened with each of the others and how they responded. Samantha kept urging them on, because any information they could give her may be able to be used to come up with a plan. Will purposely left out a few things though, and Jaden seemed to understand not to mention them as well. Samantha however, still wanted to know.

"What did your mother say, Will?" she asked as she switched the boxes in his chair. "Do you mind telling me what you tell all of them?"

Will repeated it. For some reason, he was scared to tell her. It was as if telling someone from the outside would lose the magic of it, but he continued anyway, and as he spoke, her nods and smile and even tears told him that it was okay to tell her. She was safe. He spoke quietly, as if he were talking to one of the others, but the words felt different being told to Samantha.

"Child, I love you. And God loves you. You were sent to this place because the Servants thought that you could not handle the real world. They thought you were too broken, too imperfect, to be with them and that this room would help you. But they were wrong. Friend, you are not helpless, you are not broken. The God that we follow does not make mistakes. You are perfect, just as perfect as all of the Servants, just as perfect as anyone else. You are strong, you are loved, and you are capable. You do not belong in this place. You belong in the Sovereignty. Never forget that. You can be independent. You can be powerful. You are. So, use that power to one day let the Sovereignty know that you are worthy. Get out. You can do it. You were made to show the Sovereignty what they were missing. Don't live your whole life in here. Get yourself out. Show them that you are worthy. Because you are worthy. Friend, they will see us again."

By the end, all three of them were in tears. Samantha had taken a break from switching out the boxes and stood right between Will and Jaden. She smiled through the tears. "Will," she said, looking deeply at him and seeing him in a way that no one had before. "You are so capable and so powerful. I am amazed. You did this every day? Will, you are fantastic. I don't think you realize what a huge difference that made. Honestly, Will, you are more powerful than anyone out there. You've made a bigger difference than any of the Servants, by being a *real* servant. Wow. I'm amazed by you."

Will didn't know what to say.

"Thank you, Samantha," he muttered. "It's really not that big of a thing."

"Yes Will," she countered. "It is. It really is."

Tears streamed down her face, but her smile told him that it was a positive emotion. He was glad she thought so highly of him. It felt good to have someone think that. No one ever had before.

"Can I ask you something, Will?" she said, wiping her eyes as the tears stopped flowing.

"Of course," Will said.

"Well, you told me what a lot of the people in here reacted with, but what about my girl?' she asked. "Did you do it for Victoria?"

"Yep!" Jaden said. "He did. He did."

Will looked Samantha in the eyes, "Of course I did," he told her. "but hers was a little different."

He didn't know how to tell her that the Servants had broken both of her daughter's legs and left her on the floor every day. It seemed like a terrible thing to tell someone, but he knew he had to tell her, because Victoria couldn't say it herself, and she deserved to know. He just didn't want to hurt her, when she had already done so much for him.

He started to explain slowly. Samantha walked over to Victoria and held her in her arms as much as she could through the chair. Tears streamed down her face. Will got right up to the part where the man would kick her, and he didn't want to tell her. He paused.

"Keep going, Will," Samantha said.

"I don't know, Samantha," Will shook his head, feeling her pain and anger.

"I can handle it," she told him. "I promise. I just want to know. Tell me everything. I'll be okay."

Will still wasn't sure, but he figured he would want his mom to know, so he decided to continue for Victoria's sake. Samantha, Jaden, and Will were all crying at that point, but he kept going as best he could. He explained everything up until right now, and how each day he lifts her into her seat.

"Oh, Will," Samantha came over to him. "Thank you for taking care of my girl. You have no idea how much I appreciate it."

She reached out and gave him a hug. He pushed himself up in his chair as much as he could so that they could reach each other. Her hair wrapped around his face, and suddenly he felt her warm tears on his cheek. Her tears ran down his face and shoulder. His heart melted and they both sobbed. They ached for all the injustice that had happened to Victoria and himself and all the others and the fact that he did all he could, and they still ended up in pain and neglected and unloved. It wasn't fair, and this was the first time they felt the weight of that fully together. It brought on a new depth to it that they could share in the pain, now. It hurt, but it gave them hope. Now they just needed a plan.

Samantha walked back over to the cart and finished the last chair then sat down next to Victoria, leaning her head on her daughter's lap.

"We need to do something," Will said.

"We do," she replied.

"We do!" Jaden repeated more excitedly.

"You said in the past people have been able to fight things like this by telling their story to a bunch of people, right?" Will was floating idea after idea through his head, trying to think of something.

"Yeah," Samantha answered. "That's what they did."

"So then how do we do that?"

"Honestly, I don't know." Samantha shook her head at the weight of it all and they were both struck with the reality of how hard it would be to try to get one of their stories out to the Sovereignty.

"Well, first of all, we need to figure out what we want them to know," Will said.

"They need to know exactly what your mom told you, Will," Samantha decided. "They need to see that you're capable and worthy and just like them."

"Okay, so you've got to tell them, Samantha."

"Why me?" She asked.

Will gestured toward the others.

"It can't be any of us," he said. "They won't come in, and we can't go out."

Samantha thought for a moment. Will wasn't sure what she was thinking, but he could tell she didn't want him to interrupt her thoughts. There wasn't much to think about, though. She would have to do it. Will wondered if she was thinking about doing it, or thinking about how to tell him she didn't want to. He would understand if she didn't want to mess up her life just to help him and the others. It didn't matter as much to her, because she could leave all of it behind. She could go and not look back, so why wouldn't she? Why would she try to help? It would be more work for her to stand up for them, and who knew if it would even do any good? Will waited for her to tell him all the reasons why she didn't want to do it.

"I don't think it needs to be me," Samantha said, and the look of disappointment settled on Will's face. "I think it would be better coming from you."

"Me?" Will was surprised. He couldn't do it. There were so many reasons he thought that was a bad idea, and reason after reason raced through his head as she smiled at him.

"Yeah," She confirmed. "You would be perfect. You can speak, so you'd be able to tell your story, and they would see the way you care for people and serve them and how you're no different from them, really."

"But I'm in here and they're out there," Will reminded her. "Someone on the outside will have to do it."

Samantha thought for a moment and then smiled mischievously, "Will, I really want this to work. I want justice for my daughter and justice for you and Jaden and justice for everyone in here. I want y'all to feel loved and worthy, and I think the best way to get that to happen is to have you share what you're doing in here with the Sovereignty. We just have to get you out of here."

"What?" Will asked incredibly surprised at her assertion.

"If we want you to share your story, you need to be out there in the Sovereignty for them to hear you," Samantha stood up and walked over to him. "We could do it. We could get you out!"

Will was overwhelmed. He had thought about getting out for so many years and now suddenly someone was here telling him that they could make it happen. That scared him and excited him at the same time. It was a dizzying thought. How would they do it? And what would they do once he got out? He was thinking about all of this and then suddenly realized something. He would be the only one on the outside; all the others would still be here.

"Samantha, why would you help *me* get out?" Will asked. "Why not just get Victoria out and then go home like nothing ever happened. What's in it for you?"

Samantha looked shocked. "That wouldn't change anything."

"But it would change it for you and your daughter, so what does it matter if all the rest of us are still in here?"

"It matters because y'all are part of my life now. Since Victoria was born with something different, it made me aware, and to get to her I got to you all, and now I'm here, and y'all are part of my life. Jaden and Victoria are part of your life, so the things they're going through are no longer abstract to you, now the things that cause them hurt or joy cause you hurt and joy too, right? That's why you pick Victoria up every day and why you talk with Jaden and help him learn how to speak better."

"Of course," Will answered. "I try, anyway."

"So now that you're part of my life, I want to do whatever I can to help you, because the idea of this room is no longer abstract to me. Now the things that hurt you, hurt me, and the things that cause you joy cause me joy, too. I'm all in with you, Will. I'm all in with all y'all."

Her words hung in the air and wrapped around his heart. He knew already that he would never in his life forget this conversation. This was what love was, and suddenly Will trusted Samantha in ways that he had never trusted anyone, because she loved him. She loved him enough to take on his problems and his pain, and be with him in it and help him get through it. He knew he did this as much as he could for the others, but no one had ever done it before for him. Never in his life had he felt so deeply loved.

"Thank you, Samantha," was all he could muster up the courage to say. "Thank you so much."

"No problem, Will," she said. "It's really nothing."

No, it wasn't. It was definitely something. He smiled.

"So you really want to do this?" he asked her, one final time. "You really want to get *me* out?"

"If you're sure you want to go out and you promise you'll tell your story and help fight for Victoria and Jaden and everyone else in here once you're out."

"I definitely will," he assured her.

"Then let's make it work!" Samantha smiled at Will and turned to Victoria. "We're gonna show them that you're good, Love! We're gonna get you out of here!"

Will looked at them both and smiled, whispering quietly to himself, "Yeah. Yeah we are."

Samantha whipped excitedly around.

"So how do we do it?"

Will paused. "I don't know," he said thoughtfully. "First of all, we've got to get me out of the chair."

"You said you can get out when it lays down into a bed, right?"

"Yep."

"Okay, then we wait for that."

"Won't you get in trouble?"

"Dell told me that after about a month, all the Servants will stop watching me and then I'm just on my own coming in and out. If we waited until then, it wouldn't matter if I waited in here until the beds went down because no one would be keeping track like they are now."

"Let's do that then," Will said, amazed at the idea that he could really be out of here in about a month's time.

"Sounds good. But how do we get you out? There won't be people paying much attention to me, but there are still potentially going to be out there, just waiting for their time at work to finish so they can go home."

"We could say I died," Will suggested.

"I have to document any deaths and they'll come in and remove your body. So that won't work," Samantha explained.

"True. Let's not do that then," Will flinched at the idea of them trying to remove his living "dead" body. "I think you'll have to help me get out yourself."

"You're right. That'll be the only way it'll work," Samantha agreed. "But how can we get you out without the people seeing as you go past them?"

Suddenly Jaden chimed in, "Hide and seek!" he exclaimed. "Like me and Dad!"

This was one of the first times Will had heard Jaden talk about his past. The joy in his voice really touched Will and Samantha.

"Did you used to play hide and seek with your Dad, Jaden?" Samantha asked, deeply interested, and in a voice conveying her understanding that he was completely capable of responding.

"Yes! I hide so they don't find me. Dad hide me. Dad leave. Dad come back. Dad find me. Jaden stop hiding."

"Did you hide all day?" Will asked.

"Yep. Dad at work. Jaden hide and seek. Now Will hide and seek."

"I think you're right, Jaden, I need to play hide and seek," Will decided.

"And I think I know just where you can hide," Samantha said joyfully. She ran over to the door and pulled the huge cart of boxes forward, so it was near Will, Victoria, and Jaden. She popped out the two boxes that used to be in Will's chair. They left a fairly large opening in the side of the cart.

"Could you fit in here?" She questioned, sizing him up.

"I think so," Will acknowledged. "I guess not having my legs will come in handy again!" He laughed.

"Okay, so then on the day we decide to do it, you've got to not eat, drink, or use the bathroom, so that I don't have to replace your boxes," Samantha explained, "Do you think you can do that? I can bring you some food in the day before if you want."

"That would be perfect. I can definitely do it then!" Will was surprised that they may have actually come up with a good plan.

Clearly Samantha was too. "So, we're doing this then?" She saw the agreement in Will's eyes. "I'm so excited!"

Will was excited too. At least he thought he was, but he was also really scared. He had been in here for so many years now that memories from outside were barely even clear in his mind anymore, and he didn't know what to expect. Not to mention he didn't know what he was going to do once they got him out. Or what would happen if they didn't.

"What if they catch us or figure out I'm not in my chair?" he asked.

"I won't let them figure that out," Samantha said. "I'm the only person who alerts them when something happens in here, so we'll just pretend it's all normal. And I'm sure if we do it in a few weeks, they won't be looking at what I'm doing anymore. Barely anyone did yesterday and it was my first day on the job. We'll be fine. I promise."

That comforted Will enough for now, but he still wasn't sure about one part of the plan. "What happens to all the others in here once I leave?" he asked. "What will we do about Victoria falling out of her chair, and how will all the others get socialized and touched and all of that?"

"You're right," Samantha said, disappointedly. "We need to figure something out. I can pick Victoria up, but I won't be able to switch out all the containers and spend enough time with everyone in the hour or two I'm given in here, and if I stay around too long every day, they'll think something's up."

"I do it!" Jaden exclaimed. "Will do what I do- hide and seek. I do what Will do - you worthy, they see you 'gin!"

Both Will and Samantha were instantly excited, not just because they had a plan, but because Jaden was so confident and excited about getting to do it.

"That would be perfect!" Samantha said. "Jaden, you will be wonderful at that!"

"Thank you!" Jaden's smile spread even wider.

"How are you going to get out of your chair, though, Jaden?" Will asked practically.

They all looked at each other for a second, realizing that that was definitely a problem in their plan.

"Do you know how to unlock the chairs, Samantha?" Will asked.

"I wish!" Samantha said. "But they wouldn't tell me that unless one of y'all died."

Again, they just sat in silence for a while. Waiting for someone to die could take years. Will started to let go of the idea that he was getting out until Samantha interrupted the silence.

"Let me try something," Samantha said as she walked toward the woman in the chair closest to Jaden. Will knew that the woman was pretty easy going in general. He assumed after working with her though, that she couldn't hear. Will wished he could communicate with her, but any time he made noise, she didn't react at all. He had even tried yelling, and she didn't notice. Most of their interactions just included Will sitting with her and holding her hand, but he still said the words to her, just in case.

Samantha went behind her chair and pushed forward. It didn't budge. Will knew he couldn't move them, but she might be at a better angle to do it given her height with her legs.

Eventually, with enough pushing and shoving, Samantha got the chair to move. Once it was dislodged from where it had been for so many years it started to move a bit easier. She tried to move it quickly, but it took a while until it was able to be pushed without an issue. Will wasn't sure what she was doing, and he caught Jaden's eye and he gave him a little glance saying he didn't know what was going on, either.

Finally, she moved the chair right in front of Victoria and switched their position. She then pushed her daughter over to the spot that was now empty near Jaden, and turned their chairs to face each other.

"Victoria, can you unlock Jaden's chains too?" Samantha asked, locking eyes with her daughter. Victoria gave no reply, but her hands moved from fighting her own chain to working on Jaden's.

"Perfect. Thank you, Love!" Samantha smiled and gave her daughter a kiss on the head.

"There ya go!" Samantha said. "Victoria will unlock Jaden, and Jaden will go around instead of you. What do you guys think?"

"Sounds perfect!" Will said.

"Good for me!" Jaden replied.

"Let's spend the next few weeks practicing how it will all go down, so everyone is ready for it, and then once I think it's safe, we'll set the plan in motion!" Samantha offered.

Will and Jaden's smile said it all.

Chapter Five

Seeking Freedom

The days passed quickly as Victoria, Jaden, Will, and Samantha practiced and refined their plan. There was a lot of work to be done and a lot of rearranging of details. It took a few days for Victoria to get the hang of unlocking Jaden's chair while still stuck in her own. Samantha spent a lot of time trying to tell how much longer the Servants would be keeping track of her. And Will and Jaden spent hours together working on reaching out to the others. No one thought about the fact that Jaden hadn't actually taken a step since he was locked in his chair, so the first few days that he was out ended up being a time for him and Will to practice his walking again. Day after day, Jaden worked really hard, and eventually he was able to make his way around to each of the chairs on his own. Will spent hours repeating the words to Jaden so that they made sure he had it memorized, so he could tell the others. They went around together for a few weeks, and Will showed him what the best way to interact with each of the others was.

At first, they weren't sure what to do once Jaden finished with his rounds. They tried leaving him unlocked, but without him being in the chair, it wouldn't fold down into a bed, so he couldn't sleep. The chair also wouldn't allocate the food and water if he wasn't locked in, and Samantha tried, but she couldn't sneak enough food in for him everyday. He wasn't bothered by it, though, because he knew it was what Will had done for years. Jaden was always completely comfortable locking himself back in, but everytime Will saw him do it, it made him sad because he knew that while he was gone, Jaden would still be here, locked away. He knew that it had to be him on the outside, though, because Jaden would need more training, and was just generally more timid, so he didn't even want to do it. Will watched Jaden lock himself back in everyday, and that gave him even more of a reason to want to work hard once he got out. He never wanted Jaden or any of the others to have to be locked in here ever again.

A month or so went by and things started falling into place. Eventually, the system was working perfectly. Victoria was able to unlock Jaden at the right time every day; Jaden could get out and go around to each chair, know what he was supposed to do and say for each of them, and get himself locked back in at the end. For about two weeks, the system was able to work perfectly without Will at all. He just sat back and watched, excited for what he would be doing in a few weeks, but a bit sad that they didn't need him anymore. He kept reminding himself it was good though, and that it was going to lead to something wonderful. Hopefully.

Finally, Samantha came in, about six weeks after her first day, and walked quickly straight over to Will, Jaden, and Victoria.

"I think we're ready. They haven't watched anything I've been doing for the last week. Do y'all think you're ready for this?"

"Ready!' Jaden exclaimed. "I ready! I got good at this!"

"You got really good at it, Jaden!" Will said. "I think you're ready!"

"Okay, so tomorrow, then!" Samantha said.

"Tomorrow!" Will repeated with excitement and suddenly more nerves than he expected.

"Tomorrow!" Jaden said.

Victoria smiled at them, conveying her excitement too.

"So what is going to need to happen before we get you out, Will?"

Samantha started planning.

"Well I can't eat today or go to the bathroom," Will said.

"Do you think you can do that?" Samantha asked.

"Yeah. I've been practicing a bit. I know I'll be fine without food, as long as you're able to sneak something little in for me tomorrow when you get here. The only part I'm not so sure about is the bathroom. I think I can do it, and I've been trying to practice, but I've never been able to do it quite long enough. I'm sure if I need to I'll make it work, though." Will explained. He was nervous that something would go wrong and he wouldn't be able to do it. Or, that Samantha would be scared something would go wrong, and go back on her word.

"I know," Jaden said. "Use mine! I get up, you sit down!"

"Oh! You're right, Jaden!" Will realized. "That will work perfectly. I'll just use yours. And wait for food from Samantha. Do you think you can sneak it in?"

"I think so," she said confidently. "There used to be Servants on the outside watching me come in and out and asking me if everything was okay, but now they're either gone already or just talking to each other when I come or go, so they probably won't notice if I hide something under my shirt just this once."

Will didn't realize that there might be Servants watching for him when he escaped. "So they'll be there then when we try to get me out?"

"Probably not," Samantha explained. "They're out front most mornings, but especially if I wait in here with y'all a bit longer they will have already left. By the time I leave every day they're either already gone, or they're so deep into their conversation, they're not paying attention to me. So let's just leave as late as we can and hope that they won't still be there."

"Okay," Will said, heart pounding.

"Even if they are there, they leave by the time I get the cart emptied, so I promise they won't be there when you get out."

"Okay," Will said again, a bit more comfortably this time.

"Will," Samantha said looking kindly at him. "I've got you. I promise. You trust me, right?"

"Yes," Will smiled. "I really trust you, Samantha. That's why I'm scared. I haven't trusted someone other than my mom and Jaden and myself in my entire life, and I sure haven't gotten very far trusting random Servants. But I trust you. I trust you a lot. That's terrifying, because I know you're going to take me out of here, and you're going to be the only person I have on the outside. So, I trust you, a lot, and that's the only reason I'm ready to do this. Thank you for that, Samantha."

"Thank YOU for that, Will. Thank you for trusting me. I promise I won't let you down. We're gonna do this! And we're gonna do it well!"

They all smiled at each other, but suddenly Will thought about something, "Where are we going once I get out of here, Samantha?"

"You're coming home with me. My husband and my older daughter already know. We have a bedroom set up for you already. They're excited to meet you!"

This gave Will so much more anxiety. He didn't realize he was going to have to meet people, at least not right away. This whole plan was so scary to him, which was upsetting because he knew he didn't want to be in here so it shouldn't make him nervous to leave.

"Are you okay with that?" Samantha asked, and Will realized that he had been sitting in silence.

"Yeah," Will started off quietly but then got more confident. "Yeah. That's fine. I trust you. We're gonna do this thing."

"Good," Samantha said. "I've got you, Will! It's gonna be great!"

Samantha grabbed the cart then and started switching the boxes quickly. She had forgotten she needed to do that. They were quiet, thinking, while she worked. They were both looking forward to tomorrow with so much excitement and a bit of fear. The fact that they were doing it together gave each of them enough assurance that they knew it was going to be okay.

As Samantha made it to Will's chair, he used the bathroom for the last time, and she took his boxes away.

"I'm not going to set the new ones in until tomorrow when we leave, so that there's not room to restock them in the cart tonight."

"Okay," Will said, understanding that this was the first step and that soon they would be ready to go. This time tomorrow, he'd be getting ready to leave. It was all so surreal to him, but he knew it was going to be so good.

Samantha finished the rest of the room, and Will, Jaden, and Victoria sat silently watching her and thinking. This was going to work. It had to.

After the last boxes were switched, Samantha came back over to them, "I've got to go now. I'm sorry."

"It's not your fault," Will told her.

"I wish I could stay here and help y'all get ready."

"We'll be fine," Will said. "You've got to go or they're going to watch you even more tomorrow."

"You're right," Samantha said, pulling the cart to the door. "I'm sorry."

"You're fine. Don't be sorry. It's going to change because of you. You're the last person who needs to be sorry," Will assured her.

"Thank you," Samantha smiled. "and thank you too, Jaden. You're really making this plan possible. Thank you for staying here and doing this."

"Yeah thank you, Jaden. You're wonderful," Will said, realizing he wouldn't see him again after tomorrow for who knew how long.

"Welcome!" Jaden said. "I excited!"

Samantha smiled, "And thank you too, love," she said to Victoria. "Thank you for understanding why I'm not taking you yet."

Victoria rocked back and forth, acknowledging her mom's words.

Samantha looked at all of them and started to walk to the door.

"Samantha," Will said quietly.

She turned.

"Love you," he said.

"Love you too, Will," she smiled. "See you tomorrow."

Chapter Six

Jailbreak

Tomorrow couldn't come soon enough. Will barely slept at all, and even if he had been able to have food, he probably wouldn't have been able to eat with all the nerves coursing through his stomach all at once. He had been waiting for this day for so long, never giving up hope, but at the same time not expecting freedom to come anytime soon, if at all. It was a crazy thing to think that soon he would be out of here in a world that he hadn't been a part of since he was eight years old. He was a very different person now and he was sure that even just in the last nineteen years the Sovereignty would have become a very different place, too. He hoped he had the courage to do what they were planning to do. Something stirred inside of him knowing he was planning to change the world, but not knowing how. It was the best feeling he had ever had, but it was also the worst. It was scary, and he knew it would be hard, but he hoped that it would be worth it.

The hours passed slowly, and finally it was time to execute the plan. Jaden, Will, and Victoria knew that Samantha would be there any minute. They exchanged glances, but didn't dare speak. There was something so surreal about the moment that words seemed useless.

Suddenly they heard the click of the door unlocking. Their hearts were pounding almost louder than the sound of the door. It felt like it took an eternity to open, but eventually Samantha came bouncing in.

"Hi there," she whispered, shutting the door behind her.

She walked over to Will and plopped a bag of carrots and a jam sandwich on his lap. Will smiled up at her and started unwrapping them.

The cart sat in the middle of the room, and Will couldn't take his eyes off of it. Samantha started making her rounds clicking each box in and out of the chairs. There was some unspoken rule that they couldn't start things moving until after she finished. Samantha knew she would never be able to finish if they started going right away. Each box clicked in and out with a swift rhythm and she couldn't keep from moving a bit faster today than usual. She also couldn't keep the smile off of her face. She saw that Will and Jaden couldn't, either.

Finally, she finished her rounds and pulled the giant cart back into the middle of the room. She walked over towards Will, Jaden, and Victoria with a spring in her step. She sat down, legs crossed, on the floor in front of them.

"Now we wait," she said. They couldn't start until Will could get out, so it was just a waiting game now until the chairs went down.

Will smiled at her and tried to eat a few bites of his sandwich. Jaden kept his eyes directly on Will, thinking about how he was going to take his place. He hoped he was ready. Victoria darted her eyes back and forth between her mother, Will, and Jaden. She knew what was happening and couldn't wait to find out how it went. Her spirit was warmed with the feeling that her mother and her friends had her back. It was a similar feeling to how all four of them were feeling at that moment.

"Nighty, Nighty," the chairs finally called out, and all four of them jumped.

It was time.

Will looked up at the fluorescent lights lining the ceiling for a moment thinking to himself about all the years he had spent in this place and how in a matter of moments he would be gone. Hopefully he would never be seeing these lights again. Hopefully none of them would have to for much longer.

He slid himself out of the chair, realizing that he may never have to be locked in it again. It was a freeing feeling, but at the same time, terrifying, too. He wondered just what he was getting himself into, but it was too late to turn back, and he wouldn't have wanted to even if he could.

He plopped down onto the floor and looked up at Samantha.

"Ready?" she asked.

"Yep." He moved toward the cart. "How are we gonna do this?"

"These two are open because we didn't need to refill them," she pointed to an area about the size of a microwave in the side of the cart. It went deep into the cart, though, so he realized he would have to be on his stomach. "You still think you can fit?" she asked.

"Yeah, I do. But I'll need your help," he gestured to how high it was, and then back down to himself on the ground. "You'll have to lift me in."

"Okay," Samantha said and walked closer to him.

This embarrassed Will. He wished he could have done it by himself. He was supposed to be saving all the others, and he couldn't even get in the box to save himself. Quickly he let it go, though, as she reached for him.

She lifted him as you would a child from under his arms and tried to slide him in.

"Put my waist in first," he said, "so I can still be looking out."

"Good idea."

She slid his body into the hole, and it was perfectly sized. He knew he couldn't have done it had his legs still been there, because there would definitely have not been room. Even now, it was very tight. He could only move his eyes, but not move his head or much of the rest of his body.

Looking up, he could see what was straight in front of him, but that was about all. He could see Jaden reclined in his chair, next to the empty chair that Will had been in moments before. Will watched as Jaden moved his head around trying to get it at an angle where he could see what Samantha and Will were doing.

For a split second, their eyes met. Jaden smiled. Will started to cry.

"I love you, Jaden. See you soon!" he said through tears.

"See you soon, Will. See you!"

Will's heart broke knowing that he didn't really know if he would see Jaden again soon. He might. Or something might go wrong on the outside, and he may never see him again.

"Ready?" Samantha said, looking into the hole she had shoved Will's body into as gently as she could.

"Mmhm" he vocalized. He was as ready as he'd ever be.

The cart started rolling. Will lost sight of Jaden and moved past Victoria and the rest of the others very quickly. Each time one passed, he thought of all the moments he had had with each of them. These were his friends--his family in here--and he was leaving them. He knew he was doing it so that they could have a better life, but the thought that he may never see any of them again scared him. It also scared him to think that he may be seeing them again all too soon if this doesn't go well and he just gets put back. Neither option would suffice. He knew this was their only chance, and it had to work. Otherwise no one would ever understand their worth.

The cart moved quickly and bounced a little bit every time the wheels rotated. Will could feel every curve and bump in the pit of his stomach.

"You okay in there, Will?" Samantha asked as they approached the door.

"Yep," he called back.

"We're about to leave the room, so you need to stay quiet and still. Okay?"

"Okay."

"We're going to go through the hallway, past the guard's room, but they'll hopefully already be gone, and into the supply room where all the boxes are kept," she explained. "That's when I'll make sure it's clear and help you out."

"Sounds good," he said, but he didn't feel convinced of anything.

"Will. You are going to be okay," Samantha stopped the cart for a second. "Trust me."

"I do," he said. And he did, and that made him feel a little bit better.

He saw her quickly pass around the cart to open the door and then back around to push it again. It started rolling.

"Okay," she whispered pushing it right to the edge of the room in the doorframe. "Let's go!"

She started pushing faster and Will felt the cart go over the bump of the doorframe. His heart beat faster than it ever had before and he felt it practically rattle the inside of the hole he was in. He was pressed up against the bottom and top of it so much that even the small movement of his heartbeat and breathing was hitting up against the walls. It wasn't painful, but it definitely wasn't comfortable, either.

As soon as they passed through the door, something changed. Will realized it was a change in the air. Inside their room it had been so stuffy and humid, and outside, even just in this hallway the air was so much crisper and less dense. The smell was intensely different too. It startled him how much less dank and oppressive it was. There were smells of life and nature and people, rather than decay and human waste from inside the room. He took it all in. It was a bit brighter, too. Not because the fluorescent lights were any different, but because the walls were painted white instead of grey and it was set up in a way that didn't feel chamber like, but rather open and welcoming.

All he could see was the whitewashed walls with a single blue paint stripe across what he assumed was the middle of the wall. He watched it move past him as the smells and feel of the air got even more evident the further away they went from the room.

It felt like they were rolling for hours, and Will just tried to take it all in. He was overwhelmed by it all and on top of that just simply terrified that someone might see him. They had to keep going, though, and he knew that, so he just kept watching the walls pass by, keeping quiet in his little hole.

He felt every little bump on the floor every time Samantha stopped or slowed down, even for just a second. He wondered when they would be passing the room where the guards might be. Finally, he saw a door jam and realized that must be it. Samantha stopped the cart. She was scared, too. This could be the only thing keeping them from getting Will to the world outside.

"Let's do this," she whispered unsure if it was loud enough for even Will to hear. She started pushing again. She moved the cart down the hallway quickly, trying to look unsuspicious while still trying to move fast enough that if there were guards in that room, they wouldn't see her or the opening in the cart. She walked confidently with the cart in front of her as she passed the door. Will and Samantha both looked straight ahead the whole time, hearts racing.

Once they passed the door, Samantha turned back to look and see if the guards had been there after all. Nothing. She figured that meant they were gone for the night, but suddenly she wasn't quite sure. The thought popped in her head that one of them may come back for something or still be around doing things before he or she left. Samantha knew that probably wasn't the case, but she also didn't want to risk it. Nerves built up in her chest and she couldn't stop thinking that she had to make it work or it would be her fault that Will and the all the people in the room would never get noticed.

As these thoughts raced in her head, she gave up on trying to be subtle and she broke into a run. Will was startled and not sure what was going on. He hoped there wasn't a reason she was running, or someone she was running from, but he stayed as still as he could and tucked himself as far back as possible just in case.

The cart bounced and wobbled as Samantha ran. It wasn't made to move as quickly as she was pushing it. The more it swayed, the more nervous Will got and the more he tried to hold on, but there was nothing to hold on to. He was tossed around and pushed violently up against the top and side of the cart every time it jolted. He tried not to cry out though, because he knew they needed to get there.

Samantha saw the door that led to the supply room, and she gave a final big push to get the cart in the door. As she pushed, the front wheels rolled straight into the door jam before entering the room. Samantha didn't notice though so she kept pushing. The cart wavered for a second and leaned drastically to its left. Will started to slide. He reached his hands out to try to grab for anything around him, but they simply flailed in the air as he started to go down. Samantha caught the cart and stabilized it so that it wouldn't fall completely on him. As he slid down the side of the cart, he continued to grab for something. Samantha saw him start to fall. She jumped forward around the side of the cart and leaned in as much as she could in attempts to catch him. As she leaned into grab him, his hands grasped her arm and the weight of his falling body pulled her down too.

They both hit the floor. Samantha landed flat on her back, with her arms around Will's torso. His head hit into her stomach, which knocked the wind out of her completely. They both screamed.

Samantha jumped up and grabbed the cart, pulled it into the supply room, and slammed the door. All they could do was hope that no one else was here to hear the commotion. Will sat on the floor watching her. They locked eyes and breathed as quietly as they could. Their eyes darted around the room, making sure it was all clear. After a few seconds went by, they realized no one was coming. No one had heard.

Samantha took a deep breath and leaned against the door. She let out a little laugh at how ridiculous she had been for running away from nothing. The chuckle turned into full blown giggling, and Will started laughing too. They couldn't stop. Tears ran down their cheeks as they threw their heads back in laughter.

Will saw a sparkle in Samantha's eye and she saw the same in his. He couldn't ever remember a time where he had laughed this hard, and honestly, she couldn't either. His heart was warmed, knowing that they not only were safe now, but also that they were friends. For some reason, sneaking out of the room and falling on top of each other had helped both of them get over the little bit of uncomfortable formality that still lingered between them due to their differences.

Now they were one in the same, and they knew it.

"We did it!" Samantha smiled.

"We did!" Will repeated and tears started streaming down his face. Samantha looked at him and within seconds she was crying too. Their tears turned into even more laughter.

"We can't be crying now," Samantha chuckled. "We've still gotta get you out of here. And we can't be all teary-eyed when you meet the family."

Will paused. He had forgotten that today he would have to meet people. Lots of people. To go from only ever seeing one Servant for so many years, to now knowing he was about to be back in the Sovereignty, back in a world full of them, was unbelievable. He was so excited but terrified all at the same. Something else made him pause too, though. She said "the family", not "my family". Somehow, he felt like he was part of the "the". He hoped that's why she said it that way. It gave him a warm feeling even that she would allude to the fact that it was a place for him too, and not just hers. Quickly, he decided to hold that in his mind, because he knew that this could be a very unpredictable time for him.

"Let's get out of here!" he said making his way to the door.

Samantha swung the door open and held it for him.

"After you!" she said.

"Thanks," He said sheepishly, knowing that she was already going out of her way to love him, another thing no other Servant would do.

"My car's parked right over here," she said, leading him in the right direction.

He got in the passenger seat of the self-driving car, nervous about all that lay ahead. She sat down next to him. He felt the cold leather of the seats against his back and could smell the dense car smell in the air, all things that he hadn't experienced in years. He took it all in, examining the seats and how the cars looked a bit different than they did years ago. They had always been self-driving, but these were built more dynamically. It felt different. It felt good. As the car started to move, she looked over at him.

"It's gonna be okay, you know," she said, "you being out here. You're going to love it. I promise. And we'll work as fast as we can to get every other person out of that room too, no matter how we have to do it. But, Will, I really hope you believe me when I say I've got you. Because I do. You're going to be fine. You're going to use your story to convince all the Servants that every person is worthy of a chance, no matter what differences they may have, because different doesn't mean imperfect. You're going to teach them that now. It's going to be great!"

The car pulled out of the parking lot and sped off. Will watched the building he had been confined to for so many years fade into the distance.

Chapter Seven

Welcome at the Table

The car pulled up in the driveway. Will had barely even blinked in the fifteen minute ride to Samantha's house. He was trying to take it all in--the new things that were different since he had left the Sovereignty, and the old things that he had missed for so many years. The car took them past houses, stores, schools, and countless other buildings. Each one had its near perfect outer appearance with different sizes, shapes, and colors, but not a blemish in sight. Some buildings were one story, some were two or three or even more, but all of them were flawless in outer appearance. Each had the same smooth clean walls, with beige, brown, or white paint and bright neon screen sign at the front saying the name of the store, school, or family who lived in the house. Each screen had writing in a different color to correspond to what the building held. Schools were blue, personal houses were green, stores were pink. Will tried to read them, but he wasn't able to make out what the letters meant after all these years. He had started to learn to read as a kid, and was actually pretty good at it, but now after not seeing any words for nineteen years, he couldn't remember what any of it meant. It was upsetting, but he chose not to let it get him down.

Instead, he focused on all of the things that he was seeing that re-minded him of home. He saw the turf in each of the yards, and the potted trees, bushes, and flowers that were outside some of the buildings. He knew that the Sovereignty wanted to rid the world of imperfections not only in people but also in nature, and so in the past they tried to remove any plant that didn't look exactly right. Eventually they realized that they needed the trees and other plants to live, so the Servants took it upon themselves to create "perfect" plants so that there was no dirt or falling leaves. The leaves turned colors for the seasons, but they never fell so that there would never be anything "wrong" with the area. Similar to the buildings and roads, they all were built in ways that made it so there could be no brokenness or issue with them, at least on the outside. They all looked perfect. It was comforting to Will to notice that most of the world outside had stayed the same and the standard of perfection hadn't seemed to change much. He just no longer fit into it, which hurt, but somehow, seeing all the things that he saw as a kid made him forget for a second that he didn't fit. It felt good.

He was reminded that he was imperfect as they pulled into the driveway though, because he remembered that he was going to have to meet Samantha's family now. Suddenly it occurred to him that Samantha was the only Servant that Will had ever met who didn't think about his imperfections. He was terrified now that her family would be more like the rest of the Servants he had met.

"Samantha?" he asked as the car turned itself off and unbuckled their seatbelts for them. "Are you sure this is okay?"

"Am I sure what is okay, Will?" she asked. She had let him take it all in as they drove, but it didn't surprise her that he started talking now before they got out of the car.

"Me meeting your family. Me staying here," he said.

"Of course," Samantha smiled. "We're excited to have you."

"*We*? Are you sure?" Will asked.

"Yep," she replied, "*We*--my husband, my eldest daughter, and I-- cannot wait to help you show the Sovereignty that you, Victoria, Jaden, and all the other people they call 'creatures' are just as worthy as they are. *We* are excited for you to be staying with us. *We* are excited to get to know you better."

"Okay," Will said trying to shake the fear. "Then I guess I'm excited to get to know y'all better, too. Thank you."

"Of course," Samantha said as the doors popped opened. "You ready?"

"Ready as I'll ever be," Will smiled and turned to get out of the car. He wasn't sure exactly how he was going to go about it, because he had only ever walked without legs in the room, and he knew what he was doing there, but for some reason this made him more nervous. Nevertheless, he lowered himself down out of the car and hit the ground a bit harder than he wanted to but played it off as nothing and started moving toward the door. Samantha came around the other side of the car and they started walking up to the front entrance. Will struggled to get up the step by the front door, but Samantha quickly reached out her hand and it was enough to get him up. It embarrassed him, though. The whole point of him being out here was to show the Sovereignty that he was enough, and if he wasn't even enough to get up onto a step, how would he be enough to show that to the entire Sovereignty? Again, he tried to shake it off.

Samantha reached into her shirt and took off the necklace she was wearing. Attached to it was a key that she used to open the door. The front door swung open. They both entered quietly. Will heard footsteps coming down the stairs. There were definitely two sets. A heavier one, coming later, and a bouncy lighter one moving quickly in front.

Will looked around. Directly in front of him was the staircase they were walking down. To his left was a kitchen, with a table and some of the self-cooking appliances that every house in the Sovereignty had. To his right, there was a living area with two couches, a coffee table, and a fireplace with an electric fire displayed on the screen that mechanically produced heat to warm their home. On the wall to the right of the fireplace was a mosaic glass wall-hanging. Will couldn't tell what it was a picture of at the angle he was standing. Right above the fireplace was the screen that the leader, Servant Deena, would appear on every night to talk to everyone in the Sovereignty. The house looked very similar to the one that he had grown up in, and pretty much every other house he had seen. The Sovereignty liked everything to be uniform so it could be as close to perfect as possible, but each family got to take a bit of ownership over what they kept in their homes. Even though there were a few differences, Will couldn't help but see all the similarities. It was so weird for Will to be back in one of the houses after all these years. It reminded him of home, but somehow it wasn't like the home he envisioned in his mind every day while locked away. Maybe it was that he was older now, or taller, or that he had experienced so much more.

Suddenly the footsteps got closer and the people emerged from behind the wall. The first was a girl who Will assumed was twenty seven or twenty eight, just a year or two older than himself. Her jet black hair wrapped around her face and her smile gave Will even just a glimmer of peace. She was old enough to have wisdom shown in her eyes and face, but still young enough to shine with pure joy, too. Will wondered if he had that too at this age, or if it had been stripped of him in the same way as most things in his life. Either way, it was relieving to see it now so clearly in this woman.

The next person, Samantha's husband, was a big man, both tall and wide, and he seemed to be filled with the same kind of joy and passion that Samantha glowed with now, and when Will first met her.

"Hi Will," said the girl. Their eyes met, and she gave him a little smile. He grinned back and felt jittery inside. She continued, "It's so nice to finally meet you. My mom's been telling us all about the amazing things you've done in the room and all you've done for my little sister. Thank you so, so much for caring for Victoria. I'm so glad I get to meet you," She paused and reached out to shake his hand, but instead decided to give him a hug. It felt really good, and Will thought she smelled nice.

There seemed to be a hint of earthy smells, maybe a kind of flower or something, which was hard to come by these days. "I'm Abagail by the way. Abagail Keener."

Will struggled to get the words out because he was so nervous, "Thank you, Abagail. It was really nothing. I'm so glad I was able to do something little to help your sister."

"It definitely wasn't little," the man cut in, "You probably saved our daughter's life. And now you're about to try and save countless more. I'd say that's pretty big."

"Thank you," Will smiled awkwardly up at him, not sure what to say.

"I'm Jim, by the way," he told Will. "Sam's husband."

Will was startled. Did she go by Sam?

Abagail caught what he was thinking, "Only Daddy calls Mom 'Sam'. It's been their thing since they were little. Sweet, right?"

"Yeah," Will laughed.

"Can I get you something to eat?" Jim asked, making his way over to the kitchen.

"Yeah," Samantha said. "You're probably starving! You didn't eat much of the sandwich I gave you earlier, and you couldn't eat anything yesterday."

Will hadn't thought about it, but he was actually really hungry. So much had been going on that he didn't even think about the fact that the only food he had eaten in the last 24 hours was a few bites of a sandwich.

"Sure," he answered. "I'd really appreciate that."

"What kind of foods do you like, Will?" Abagail asked.

Will stopped, "Oh... I guess I don't really know," He hadn't thought about that either, "We just got our little food patties in the room, so I haven't had anything real since I was eight. I'm not really sure what I like. Sorry."

"Don't say sorry!" Abagail said laughing and shaking her head. "It's not *your* fault!"

"True, I guess," Will said shyly.

"Guess we'll just have to try out a bit of everything and figure out what you like now!" Samantha said.

All four of them sat down around the table. Will pulled himself up in the chair and looked around at the three people sitting around him. Tears formed in his eyes. He was finally, for the first time in nineteen years, doing something that a real person would do, and it felt so good. A piece of the hurt surrounding his heart in those nineteen years fell away and he felt loved even just a little bit, for the first time in a long time by people other than the others in the room with him. It made him tear up to know that all three of these people were on his side and willing to fight for him.

Jim stood up and walked over to the counter. He pressed the little buttons it took to start making dinner. After a few minutes they decided on just having a pizza, so Will could try something that he would probably like. The kitchen got to work and started making the pizza. Jim had to push a few buttons along the way, but other than that the kitchen was completely self-sustaining and able to make the food for them. Will remembered watching every night when he was young what the kitchen would do to make their food at home.

The pizza finished in a few minutes and the plates came out full of pizza, salad, fruit, and a cookie for dessert. Will was so excited for real food. After so many years with the same thing, it was almost overwhelming to know that he had so many options on one plate tonight. Jim grabbed the plates and passed one to him first and then to his wife and daughter and took the last one for himself.

They sat there and talked for a while. Mostly they caught Will up on what had changed while he was gone.

"So Servant Deena is still in power?" Will asked them all.

"Yep," Jim said and they all shook their heads.

"What?" he asked, confused.

Jim started to explain, "We just wish we had someone as a leader who chose to be, well..."

"An actual servant," Abagail finished bluntly, and then explained to him, "It's just so hard knowing she calls herself that, but still does things that are so unfair to people like you and my sister, and even does things that are unfair to the people around her. Everyone just writes it off as her trying to be perfect, but it's more important to have perfect love than individual perfection in our opinion."

"Yeah," Samantha said. "She says she's a servant, but she gets to assign the jobs and timing of things and where people go and what they do and how they look, and it's supposed to lead to perfection, but it just leads to uniformity. Uniformity isn't perfection. It's just sameness. Perfection is love."

"Servant Deena definitely doesn't understand that," Jim said. "Nor do any of the other Servants, really, so that's why we choose to avoid being called a Servant."

"So you all don't want to be called 'Servant'?" Will asked.

"Definitely not," Abagail said exasperatedly. "Mom and Daddy gave me the choice of whether I wanted to or not, but every time someone says it by accident it bothers me so much. I'd rather be a servant for real than be called a Servant by Servants who only serve themselves."

"Oh wow," Will was stunned. He had never heard anyone say anything like that, "Do other people do that too, now?"

"No, pretty much still just us," Samantha said.

"That's amazing," Will said. He had always wanted to be called a Servant, because he was never allowed to be, but this made so much sense to him now. He thought back to all the times he had heard his mom and dad get called Servant as a kid. It was just what people did, but he wondered if they were really serving others, or just themselves. He knew his mom had served others, simply by telling him the affirmations he passed on to so many others, but he wondered if that was intentional. Suddenly he realized he hadn't even asked about her yet at all.

"Um... do any of you happen to know my mom? Her name is Grace Josephs. And my Dad is Xavier Josephs. Do you know them? I want to know if they're okay."

"You know, Will, I don't think I do," Jim thought for a second.

"Me either," Samantha said. "But we could find them."

"Oh you're right," Jim jumped out of his seat. "Let's do it."

They all got up and walked quickly over to the wall with the big screen on it. Will knew from when he was younger that when Servant Deena was not being broadcasted on it, it worked as the families' giant touch screen computer. There was a registry with everyone in the Sovereignty listed in it, so he could finally know if his parents were still okay.

Samantha started taping the screen and searching for his parents' names. Quickly, their pictures popped up on the screen and their information was displayed beside it. It gave their ages, names, place of employment, and their address.

"They live 34 kilometers from here," Jim noted. "We could try to go visit them at some point."

Will didn't comment. He had noticed something else as Samantha kept scrolling.

They all stopped talking and stared at the screen. Will's heart started pounding and there was an empty feeling in his chest. Under the place for their address, it gave a space for relatives. It listed their parents and siblings first, and then their relation to each other. Under the Spouse category, it said "Children." None of them could believe their eyes. This was even a new low for the Servants, because instead of even acknowledging the eight years Will was in the Sovereignty, let alone the 26 years he had been alive, their information simply said, "Children: None".

"I'm sorry, Will," Abagail put her hand on Will's shoulder. "I'm so sorry."

"It's okay," Will whispered, trying to hold back tears full of both sadness and anger.

"No," Samantha said. "No, it is most definitely not okay."

She clicked around some more on the computer and pulled up her and Jim's information. Theirs too, had been changed without them knowing. It said, "Children: Abagail Keener", and on Abagail's page it said, "Siblings: None." Will and Victoria's presence had been wiped clean from the world without even a second thought. That was not only hurtful, it was just completely incorrect. Everyone who tried to get information about them were receiving false information. Grace and Xavier Josephs did in fact have a child; Samantha and Jim Keener did have two daughters; and Abagail Keener did have a sister, but this directory, that everyone counted on and used daily, was just plain wrong. It had wiped them completely out of history.

Samantha started searching for Will and Victoria's pages individually, but all that came up was a one word error message:

"Imperfections."

"They delete you from the system and all they call you are 'imperfections'?" Abagail said forcefully. "That's despicable. That's disgusting. That's not fair."

"That's imperfect," Samantha whispered, and they all chuckled with sad hearts. "Literally, they put false information into the system and into our heads. Not having this knowledge is imperfect. Providing false facts is imperfect. *You* are not imperfect. The Sovereignty is. That's as plain as day right here."

"You're right, Mom," Abagail nodded. "I can't believe how many people can't understand that."

"Me, either," Will and Jim said quietly at the same time.

Samantha brought Will's parents back up on the screen. They read through all their information. It gave every place they'd ever worked, everyone they knew and how they knew them, and other detailed information about who they were. But it said nothing about their son.

"What do you want to do, Will?" Samantha asked.

"About what?"

"About your parents," she explained. "Do you want to visit them? Or stay with them? Or get them involved in our plan? I understand if you would."

"I don't," Will said quickly without even thinking. He just knew he couldn't and the more he thought about it the more he realized he really couldn't. It wasn't that he didn't want to, he just knew it wouldn't work. "I think if I do, I wouldn't go through with this. I think I'd just want to hide and be with my family forever. If this works, then I'll get to be with them. I shouldn't get to before Victoria gets to be with you and Jaden gets to be with his family and all the others get theirs. It would be so hard to keep focused on that if I were with them. Does that make sense?"

"Completely," Samantha said. "Thank you for being willing to do this all, Will. It's a lot to ask of you, but it's so worth it."

"It definitely is," Will said, hoping it was true. Hoping that in the end, after whatever happened was done, he would still believe it was true.

Suddenly, the screen started to change. Servant Deena's face appeared on it.

"Will! Get down!" Samantha called. He dropped to the floor. The three of them ran over and sat on the couch facing the screen. Will slid himself back against the wall underneath the screen so he was facing them. He knew that when Servant Deena came over the T.V., it scanned the room to make sure the right number of eyes were watching her the whole time. It came on at the same time every day, so everyone knew they had to be in their houses at that time or officers would track them down and bring them home. Will wasn't sure what would happen if it registered an extra pair of eyes in their house that didn't belong anywhere else, but he didn't want to find out, so he laid on the floor under the screen as still as he could. The screen registered each pair of eyes and beeped three times, announcing that it had logged them in its system.

"Good evening, Servants!" Servant Deena started. "I trust you all are well."

Will could see the reflection of the television in the glass mosaic piece behind their heads on the wall behind the couch. He remembered what she looked like from when he was a kid. She had barely changed at all, except today her dark, wavy hair was tied up in a ponytail, when in the past she had had it down around her shoulders. Will remembered thinking it looked fun to play with because it was so fluffy. Now though, it disgusted him knowing she was a good part of the reason he and so many others had spent most of his life locked away. Watching her made him upset, and the things she was saying didn't make it any better.

"I have a few wonderful updates for you tonight that I am sure you will all be overjoyed to hear." She went on, "First of all, I want to tell you what our scientists have been working so diligently on today. They have made an astounding breakthrough yet again. In the last few days, scientists all over the Sovereignty worked together to make another improvement to each and every one of our lives. Today they want me to let you know how hard they are working to learn how to control the sky and what it looks like."

Will knew that a long time ago people found a way to control what the weather was, when and where it rained and snowed, and how to make those things stop in most areas so that nothing would get dirty. Generally though, the color of the sky has just been something that has not caused any point of issue, but Will guessed that the Sovereignty will probably be excited that yet another thing in their lives will be "perfect." Samantha was right; apparently to them, uniformity was perfection, and if even the clouds and color of the sky had to be uniform and controlled, he worried about how hard it would be for the Sovereignty to accept that people don't need to be.

"This change will take place in the next few months if they can help it, and for the rest of time, our sky will be controlled to look how we want it to."

"A second update for y'all is in the department of education. We want to share with you that we continue to make strides in teaching each person to be a little more perfect each day. In schools around the Sovereignty today, many of the students took their second Sovereignty-assessment of the year."

Will remembered taking two or three of those Sovereignty-assessments as a kid. He had gotten full marks after answering questions about basic historical events, easy math facts, and ways to increase personal growth towards perfection. Every student had to take it until they received a perfect score, although most of them got it right away because they were things that the Sovereignty had drilled into them since they were born.

"All of the teachers reported back the scores today, and yet again, every child scored perfectly and has learned what it means to be growing into the flawless image of God. We will test again, as we always do, two more times this year to make sure that each young person is getting an education to instruct them in all the right ways."

"Our last update for the day is about the government. I would just like to remind you that I am here for you. I am in this position to lead you closer to the best you can be. I am thankful for this opportunity to help you help yourselves. Today I would like to leave you with a quote from our last greatest Servant, which says, 'God created people in God's image, an image of perfection, and the more we show that image the closer to God we become. When we are one with God we are one with ourselves and those around us. Perfection leads to godliness, and godliness leads to contentment, comfort, knowledge, and power. Strive for greatness, for that is what God created you to do.'"

Will saw Samantha, Jim, and Abagail all shake their heads. They were definitely not a fan of what message this woman was giving them. They exchanged looks of disgust and Will shared in their discomfort. Finally, Servant Deena closed her statements.

"Now, it is time for the pledge to our Sovereignty, ourselves, and our God. Then I will say goodbye for the night. Ready, begin..."

All three people sitting across from Will stood up and put their right hand on their heart and their left hand behind their back. The screen beeped three times again, registering each person's compliance with the way they were to recite the pledge. Will was stunned though, because Samantha, Jim, and Abagail all stood silently. Honestly Will didn't know that that was an option. He and his family as a kid had always said the pledge, but he was glad that these people chose not to participate. They stood in silence and listened to Servant Deena recite the pledge on the screen.

"I pledge to the Sovereignty that I will strive to make it as good as it can be. I pledge to the Servants in charge to follow in their lead for me. I pledge to myself that I will be defined by my perfection. I pledge to God to try to be perfect until God's perfect will is done."

The screen went black. Samantha looked at Will and gave him a smile saying it was okay to get up. He stood and joined them on the couches.

"You don't say the pledge?" Will asked.

"No," Abagail explained. "We don't agree with it or what it stands for, so we choose not to say it."

"You can do that?" Will was surprised.

"No one knows if we're doing it or not," Jim told him. "they just make sure our hands are on our hearts."

"Oh. I guess you're right," Will realized. "I never thought about that. I like that."

"Me, too," Samantha said looking proudly around at her family. Suddenly she realized the time. "Will, we should show you where you're going to sleep and everything. You haven't even seen upstairs yet."

All four of them got up and made their way up the stairs. Will was a bit nervous about how he was going to get up, but by holding onto the railing and wall he was able to pull himself up each step without any help at all, even though Samantha did offer.

They reached the top of the stairs and Will looked around. As he expected, it looked pretty similar to every house he had been in. The walls were the same light brown color and the rooms were laid out in a similar way. There was a hallway as he got to the top of the stairs, and to the right were two individual bedrooms, to the left was the master bedroom, and next to that was the bathroom.

Jim led them all into the small bedroom to the right. "This is your room for now," he explained. Will looked around and saw a bed, a dresser, a closet, and some decorations on the wall. In the midst of the decorations was a big letter "V". Suddenly he realized where he was.

"This is Victoria's room," he noted.

"Yep," Abagail confirmed. "We've kept it ready for when she can finally come back to us."

"I don't have to sleep here," Will said. "I can sleep on the couch downstairs or something. I don't want to take her room."

"It's fine," Abagail assured him, and Samantha added, "You're fighting to get her back here. If anyone deserves to stay in the room until she gets back, it's you."

Jim and Abagail nodded in agreement.

"Thank you all," Will said, honored.

"We've put some clothes and pajamas for you in this drawer." Jim opened the dresser and showed him his things, "and here are things to brush your teeth and do your hair and any other stuff we could think of that you'd need. Let us know if you need anything else."

Will surveyed his new belongings. He hadn't come with anything other than the hospital-like gown that he had been in for the last many years in the room, so to have all of these things was wonderful. "Thank you so much," he said again.

"Of course," Samantha said. "Thank you."

"Yeah," Abagail said. "Thank you so much for being willing to do all of this and come out here and live with people you barely even know so that you can help save lives. You should be the one being thanked."

Will smiled up at her not sure what to say. Her eyes met his and her smile felt like something special. He felt seen, not just by Samantha, but now by Abagail too, and Jim.

Samantha broke the silence, "Well, it's getting late. We should probably all try to get some sleep now, so that we can start talking about a plan tomorrow. Sound good?"

"Definitely," Will agreed.

"Let us know if you need anything, Will, okay." Jim told him.

"Okay," Will said, "Goodnight!"

"Goodnight, Will," Abagail said and then her mother and father repeated it. Will remembered the last many years of his life and how every night, he and Jaden said goodnight to each other, and the chairs echoed their condescending goodnights at them as well. He was sad thinking that there would be no one to tell Jaden goodnight tonight, but he was also thankful to have so many people bid him goodnight tonight and that he didn't have to listen to the chairs say goodnight to him at all.

Samantha, Jim, and Abagail's "goodnight's" were so much better.

Chapter Eight

Clearly Known

Will tossed and turned in his bed all night. This was the first time in nineteen years he was in a real bed, with real pajamas, and without the noises and smells surrounding the others. It was also the first time that he tried to sleep during the actual night, not during the day sitting up in his chair so he could make his rounds when the chair went down. Because of all of this, he was barely able to sleep at all. His mind was racing from the events of the day, and his body still was not used to being out of the chair and in a real house with real freedom to do things that he wanted. It overwhelmed him, and even though he was tired, he lay awake staring at the ceiling.

Turning to look at the clock, he saw it was two in the morning, and he had barely fallen asleep at all. He was comfortable lying there though, on a real mattress in one of Jim's pajama shirts in a house belonging to people who so clearly loved him. That was something that he had hoped for the entire time he was in the room, so knowing he was here now experiencing it, was really enough to keep him awake by itself. He was so happy he was here, but he was also terrified about what was to come and what he would need to do.

These thoughts raced through his head as he lay there. He looked around the room examining all of Victoria's things, and thinking about the life that she had lived here and the life that she would get to live here if everything went the way he was hoping it would. He noticed something interesting on the door and laughed right away. After a few seconds of thought, he got up to go look more closely at it. As he walked up to the door, his suspicion was confirmed. There were multiple broken locks on the side of the door, lining almost the entire thing. He laughed again, because he knew that they needed to keep Victoria hidden while she was here, but he also knew her innate ability to unlock things, so he could clearly picture her breaking out of here every day.

Since he was up, he figured he'd make his way to the bathroom. He didn't want to share this with Samantha or her family, but it was weird for him to remember when he needed to use the restroom, because for most of his life, it was just under him, so he never had to think about it. Obviously, he knew he couldn't do that here, but sometimes he forgot it was something he needed to pay attention to. Once he got out, he looked back at the bed, but realized that he had too much energy to lay back down again. He figured he might as well go get something to eat or drink since he was already awake.

Carefully and quietly, he made his way to the stairs, trying as hard as he could not to do anything that would wake up anyone else in the house. He grabbed onto the railing and pulled himself down each step one by one, using his arms and the railings to hold himself up more than trying to balance on the bit of his legs or his torso somehow. Doing it that way made it quieter, too, so he was almost making no noise at all. He quickly got to the bottom of the stairs and turned to move towards the kitchen.

As he turned, he saw a silhouette of someone sitting on the couch, and realized he wasn't the only person awake.

"Hi, Will," the person said quietly, in attempts not to scare him. It didn't work though. Will was terrified. His first thought was that it was a Servant from outside the house who had come to take him back to the room. He realized that was crazy, but his instinct was still to turn around and start back up the stairs.

"No, Will, You're fine. You can come down here if you want. It's just me."

Will turned around again and looked to see who the person was.

"Hi, Abagail," he said quietly.

"You couldn't sleep, either?" she asked him.

"Definitely not," he laughed.

"I don't blame you. There has been so much going on for you today. I'm so impressed with how well you're handling it," she told him. He could barely see her smile through the darkness between them.

"Thank you," he said, and then he admitted, "It has been a lot. I am so incredibly thankful that y'all opened your house to me and are planning to help me and the other's get out of the room for good. It means a lot, but honestly this is all still so overwhelming."

"I bet," Abagail said. "It must be absolutely crazy. I can't even imagine."

"Yeah. It definitely is," Will said, and tried to bring it back to something else again. "And not to mention, I haven't actually slept at night, or lying down, in the last nineteen years, so trying to sleep tonight isn't exactly a typical thing for me."

"Oh yeah," Abagail acknowledged. "My mom was telling me all about what you did in there every night. That's really amazing, Will."

"I'm sure you would have done the same thing if you were in my position," he said, and he meant it.

"I really hope I would have," Abagail said thoughtfully. "What was it like, Will? Do you mind me asking?"

"Not at all," Will said; he was actually excited to get to share with her all of the things he experienced in the room over the nineteen years. He hoped that she really wanted to know. He walked over toward where she was sitting on the couch, so that he could tell her all about it.

"Here," she motioned to the spot next to her. "Come sit down."

"Okay," he said, pulling himself up on the couch next to her. She smiled at him and waited for an answer to her question.

"You really want to know what it was like?" Will asked.

"Definitely," she said. "Anything that you want to tell me."

"We might be here all night then," he laughed, but she didn't laugh with him.

"Okay," she said completely seriously. "If you want to tell me it all, then I'd sit here all night every night. The Servants took your life away from you for no reason other than that you're different from them. The least I could do is listen to what it was like. I want to know about you, Will. Who are you? What have you been through these past nineteen years? And what was your life like before that? Where did you come from? I want to know you, Will. I want to know your story, so I can help fight for you and for my sister and everyone else in that room, and the more I know, the more I understand. But I also want to know you for you. If you're going to be staying with us for a while, I want to know who you are."

Will was struck silent for a second, "I don't think I know who I am, honestly," He realized aloud, "I think they took that away from me right when they put me in that room. I didn't get to know who I was for nineteen years because I was strapped to a chair. I had so little freedom, there was no way to figure out who I was. I was just a prisoner."

"I'm so sorry, Will," Abagail said, putting her hand on his shoulder. "I'm so sorry that people stripped that basic right away from you. It's your right to know who you are, and they took that away without a second thought."

"They did," Will had never thought about it this way, but the thought was sobering. It hurt him to realize just how little he really knew about who he was. "I could answer your question about other people. I could tell you who my mom and dad were. I could tell you who Samantha is. I could even probably tell you a bit about who you are. But I can't tell you much about who I am, or who any of the others are either. I can tell you what's happened to us, though. I can tell you what they did to me."

"Then tell me that, if you want," Abagail prompted him. "And then maybe, we can use this time that you're here to figure out just exactly who you really are. I can help you if you'd like."

"I'd love that," he admitted. "I would really love that. I want to know who I am, and I'd love it if you could help me figure it out."

"I'd love that too, then," Abagail said. "And maybe in the process we can learn a bit about who I am, too."

"I would love that, too," Will smiled.

"Thanks," Abagail smiled back and they paused, looking at each other for a bit longer than Will expected. After realizing they hadn't spoken in a few moments, Will pulled his eyes away from Abagail's and she jumped up. "I'm so sorry, I never even asked, do you want some tea or something?" she said awkwardly.

"Yeah," he said matching her tone. "Tea would be great."

"You can try our peach tea. It's my favorite kind," she told him as she started pressing the buttons that would eventually make them two mugs of tea, with the perfect amount of cream and sugar already added.

They didn't speak as the kitchen made the tea, and as soon as it was done, Abagail grabbed them both and met Will back at the couch. She handed him his tea, set hers down on the coffee table, and sat back down next to him, this time a little closer.

"You want to know one of the worst parts of being in there?" Will asked as he tried his tea.

"Sure," Abagail said, not sure what she was in for.

"All we were ever given was dense, brown food patties, that had all the nutrition we needed but no flavor, and then a few times a day the chairs squirted water in our mouths. I haven't had real food in nineteen years."

"That's awful," Abagail agreed.

"Yeah, but it's crazy because I never even really cared. All I cared about was getting out and getting to see my family. Even when I made my rounds and connected with all of the others, most of the time I was thinking about my mom. Most of the time, all I really thought about was getting out, and now that I'm out, I'm realizing all of the little things that I didn't even think about while I was in there, and how those were really all the big things because they were what made me feel less human. Those little things--those are the worst part."

"I'm sorry Will," Abagail didn't know what else to say.

He continued, "Now I realize that it's the things like never getting a full night's sleep, and the condescending voices of the chairs, and the lack of food, and the way we were strapped to toilet chairs. All of those things were huge, but none of them felt like anything after being taken away from my home and my life and the people I loved."

"That makes sense," Abagail tried to understand. "I bet it really didn't matter when all you wanted was to be loved and every little thing the Servants put you through made you feel like you weren't loved at all."

"Exactly," Will said. "And I would go around telling all of the others that they were so loved, and now Jaden is probably doing that as we speak, but every aspect of each of our lives was out of a place of being completely unloved by the world around us."

"Will, do you know that's not true?" Abagail asked.

"Do I know it, or do I feel it?" he asked. "Because I know it in my head. That's what I've told all the others about each other and about myself for years. But do I feel loved? Not really. No one was ever even given the opportunity to look past my differences and imperfections and even know that there was a person there to love."

"I see your differences, Will," Abagail noted. "But I don't see them as imperfections. And I see you, Will. I see there is a person, a unique person, a different person, but still a person who completely deserves to be loved. I know you say you don't know who you are, but I know that you are brave, because you're out here fighting for your rights, and you're strong, because you made it through all those years and you came out, still able to be positive, and you're kind, because you spent all your time in that room showing others how loved they are. That's what I see in you, Will. I see you're different, and brave, and strong, and kind. I see the person that the Servant's don't see, and Will, I love that person. I love you."

"I love you too, Abagail," Will said. "And I don't just love you because you took me into your home. I love you because you see me, and you see your sister, and you've spent years fighting for her. I love you because you don't do what all the other Servants do because it's easy, but instead you stand out and do what's really right. I see your differences too, and your bravery and your strength and your kindness. I love you too, Abagail."

Will didn't realize that as they spoke, their voices got quieter and they learned in closer and closer to each other until they were practically touching. As Will finished speaking, his words were barely audible, and Abagail could just make them out. He speech was slower too, and as he slowed down, they both barely noticed he got to the end of what he was saying. Their eyes met and this time, neither of them pulled away. They looked at each other intently for a while, and Abagail put her hand on Will's shoulder again. Will did the same to her, and then he moved it slowly up to stroke her cheek. As he did this, they leaned in closer, closing the few centimeters of space between them. Her lips touched his gently and their bodies leaned into each other, holding each other up. As they kissed, they both held each other full of the joy of knowing they were loved and known by another person. They were seen for something more than anyone else saw in them. Will smelled the floral fragrance of Abagail's hair and face, and Abagail felt the touch of his smooth skin. Slowly, after a few seconds that felt like hours, they moved back away from each other, but just slightly enough to meet each other's eyes again.

"I love you, Will," Abagail whispered.

"I love you too, Abagail," Will whispered back. They leaned in and held each other in a hug.

"Thank you for tonight," Will said, "Thank you for seeing me."

"Thank you for seeing me, Will," Abagail said, and he knew she meant it. They both felt more known by each other than they had ever felt by anyone before.

After a while, they both sat up. "We better be getting to bed," Abagail said. "We have to figure out a plan tomorrow. It's gonna be a big day."

"Yeah, we probably should," Will agreed standing up.

"Here," Abagail said, taking Will's mug and grabbing her own off the table, both still full of tea. "I'll put these away."

"Thanks," Will said as he made his way to the stairs. He started walking up, but then turned back after a step or two. "Abagail. I never asked. Why are you up?"

"I'm up a lot every night," she admitted, "It started when Victoria left. I couldn't stop thinking about what could have been happening to her. I still can't. But tonight, I was thinking about something else too."

"What were you thinking about?"

"I was hoping I'd get to see you."

Chapter Nine

New Plans

After the kiss, Will didn't even think about the possibility of falling back to sleep. He sat on the bed full of so many emotions that he could barely think at all. Not only was he overwhelmed by the day and each of the new things that he hadn't experienced in nineteen years, or in some cases at all, but now he was also overwhelmed by the feelings he had for Abagail. He had loved other people in his life: his mom, his dad, Jaden, many of the others, Samantha. But something about Abagail was different. It was deeper and they knew each other in a way that he never thought he could know or be known, yet they had only actually known each other for a matter of hours. There was something special about it, though, and there was no denying that. He sat in those feelings, not even thinking anything, just feeling for the two or three hours left before everyone else would be up.

Once Will noticed that it was seven o'clock, he started to put clothes on. They were Jim's clothes, of course, because all he had was the gown he wore for most, if not all, of his nineteen years in the room. He wasn't exactly sure what happened to the gown, but he hoped Samantha had gotten rid of it. It was weird to be in real clothes again, though. They were tighter, softer, and thicker than Will remembered, but he liked it. It felt like home when he was a kid.

After about ten minutes, he started to hear that the rest of the house was up and tinkering around downstairs, so he decided to join them. He made his way down the stairs, which was getting easier and easier the more he practiced it.

"Morning, Will!" Samantha called. She was sitting on the couch with a cup of tea and what looked like some toast. Jim was sitting at the table eating a muffin with some jam, and Abagail was sitting across from him, drinking tea out of the same mug she had last night.

"Good morning," he said to all of them. He met Abagail's eyes for a second, and she smiled at him. He smiled back, and he felt it all the way through his body. It was a small enough interaction that neither Samantha nor Jim noticed at all. Will gave both of them a little smile, too. Quite honestly, he was surprised because he had figured at least for the first little bit of his stay here it would be a bit awkward between all of them, but since he arrived yesterday, he felt nothing but welcomed and loved. It was like there was no difference and that he had just always been around. He liked that feeling of comfort.

"So," Jim asked Will. "You ready to get to work figuring out what our plan's going to be?"

Abagail cut in before Will could answer, "Geez, Dad! Let him get something to eat first. He just woke up!"

"You're right," Jim admitted. "Sorry, Will. I'm just so excited to figure out what we're going to do!"

"It's all good. I am too!" Will said as he sat down with them at the table. Samantha joined them then, after grabbing something off the counter.

"I had the kitchen make some pancakes for you, Will," Samantha explained, setting down a warm plate of pancakes in front of him. She drizzled sweet smelling syrup all over them. "Thank you!" He smiled up at her, excited to start eating. It was delicious. Definitely the best tasting thing he had had since getting out of the room. He ate the entire plate in just a few minutes and they all laughed when he realized how fast he had done it.

Right as he finished, the screen started making noise, and Servant Deena's face appeared for the morning announcements. The four of them ran into the other room; Samantha, Jim, and Abagail sat on the couch and Will dove on the floor underneath the T.V. again.

Will only listened a bit as Servant Deena told the Sovereignty the weather, the scripture of the day, and her update saying how she was there for them. Mostly, he lay on the ground looking up at the three people on the couch. They had to keep their eyes on the screen the whole time, so they didn't see Will staring. He looked up at them with loving eyes. It hurt him a bit to watch them all have to stare at this woman whom he knew they could not stand because they felt she was hurting them and Victoria. As he watched them, he saw in them their drive to change all that was going on and to make a difference. He could almost visibly see the love in their eyes and in their body language. Will hoped he could be like these people he was watching.

He was startled when they stood up. Apparently, he had missed the fact that it was time to say the pledge because he was so deep in thought. He listened to Servant Deena alone speak the words, "I pledge to the Sovereignty that I will strive to make it as good as it can be. I pledge to the Servants in charge to follow in their lead for me. I pledge to myself that I will be defined by my perfection. I pledge to God to try to be perfect until God's perfect will is done." It was so powerful to Will that she was the only one talking. The silence of everyone else in the room somehow seemed louder than the words she was saying. He smiled to himself, glad that he was with these people who knew how to stand up for justice.

As Servant Deena finished the pledge, the screen turned off and all four of them made their way back over to the table. Once they sat down, Samantha turned to Will.

"So, Will, are you good hanging out for a few hours while the three of us go to our jobs? We'll try to get done pretty quickly so we can all get back and make a plan."

"Yeah, that's fine," he said, and then he quickly added, eyes filling up with tears, "Will you tell Jaden and Victoria I say I miss them and I love them?"

Samantha noticed he was trying not to cry, and that made him feel better. "Of course, I will," she said. She grabbed her bag off of the coffee table and got ready to go.

"Thanks," Will whispered, because that was all he could get out. Jim and Abagail grabbed their bags too, and made their way to the door.

"Okay, we'll be back as soon as we can!" Abagail said.

"See you later," Will waved, and they walked out of the door. He was by himself. For a few minutes he just sat there, not sure what to do, but finally he figured it would probably be a good idea for him to try to get some rest since he hadn't actually slept more than an hour or two in the last day. At first, he went up to Victoria's room, and laid down on the bed. He still found it hard to sleep there, though, because he hadn't slept lying down for years. After trying for a while, he decided it'd be easier to sleep sitting up. He went back down again and sat on the living room couch. In a matter of minutes, he was asleep, and he didn't wake up until he heard the door start to open.

Will realized that a few hours had passed, and Samantha was back. She came and sat down with him on the couch.

"Jaden says hi," she told him. "And he loves you, too."

"Thank you, Samantha," he said. "Are they all okay?"

She sighed, "As much as they were when you were in there. Victoria got Jaden unlocked and he went around last night to each of the people and spoke your words."

"My mom's words," he corrected her.

"True," she admitted. "Other than that, everything was about the same."

"Okay. That's good, I guess," Will said. "Well, not good, but at least doable."

"Yeah," Samantha agreed, "but the longer I spend in there with Jaden and Victoria and everyone, the more I know that we have to figure this out quickly. We need to do something now."

"Definitely," Will nodded.

At that, Jim and Abagail both came through the door. They all greeted each other with hugs and hellos and they sat down in the living room again.

"So," Jim asked. "Are we ready to figure this out?"

They all laughed.

"I sure am!" Will said.

"Okay! Let's do this then," Samantha said. She stood up and had the kitchen put out some sodas for all of them and she brought them over.

"I actually had an idea today about what we could do," Will admitted, "but it's kind of strange."

"Let's hear it," Jim said. "I think we need a bit of strange with this, 'cause if not, nothing's ever going to get done."

Will agreed and he started sharing his idea. "So while Servant Deena was speaking today, I was looking up at y'all from the ground, and I thought it was so upsetting that you were all forced to watch her, even though you clearly don't believe and agree with anything she was saying."

"Yeah," Abagail commented. "It's so upsetting, because I'm sure it's not just us. There are so many people being forced to watch something that they don't agree with, or that they don't even know they shouldn't agree with."

"Exactly," Will agreed. "But as I was watching you, I realized that just like y'all don't want to hear what Servant Deena says, most of the people who need to hear my story and who need to hear about what happens in that room won't want to hear what I'm saying."

"You're probably right, Will," Samantha agreed. "People always say that they're sorry to hear that I got assigned to work with y'all in there, but I'm not sorry. They don't realize they shouldn't be, either. They don't know what they're missing, and if I try to tell them, they don't want to hear it."

Will nodded, "So they're definitely not going to *want* to hear from me: someone with an imperfection."

"Yeah," Jim said sadly. "They probably aren't."

"But y'all don't *want* to listen to Servant Deena, and you still do," Will pointed out. "You might not agree with a single second of it, but you are still taking it in and at least hearing her words."

"True," Abagail replied. "So what are you saying?"

"I think we need to force them to listen," Will asserted. "Even if they don't take it in at first, if they are forced to listen to what we're saying, then they can't not hear the words of the story, and to some extent after just hearing it, they'll internalize it and hopefully realize that the Sovereignty is wrong. I think forcing them to hear is our only chance to get them to listen."

"That makes sense," Jim realized. "You're right. That's the only way they'd even take the time to hear it."

"That's what we need to do, then," Samantha agreed.

They sat in silence for a while realizing Will was right and thinking about all it would entail. Will finished his soda and set it on the coffee table. Abagail's eyes caught his, and she gave him a sad smile because she knew how hard this was going to be.

"So, how do we do that then?" Abagail asked Will and her family, looking around at them to see what they were thinking.

"Exactly like Servant Deena does," Samantha said matter-of-factly.

"Yeah," Jim agreed. "We need to force them to hear us just like they're forced to hear her."

"No," Samantha laughed. "Like *exactly* like Servant Deena does."

"Oh," Jim said seriously. "How?"

"Will," Samantha looked at him directly instead of her husband. "I think we need to get you on that screen."

Will froze.

"What?" Abagail asked surprised.

"Will was right. The only way to make them hear is to force it on them, and the best way to force it on them is to use the model of forced information that's already set up. We need to get him on that screen so everyone watching will see him and hear him and know what he's gone through. If we can make that happen, then I'm sure they'll see that he is just as perfect as everyone else, and then they'll know that this has to stop."

Everyone was staring straight at Samantha, their eyes barely wavering. Will thought his idea was a bit out there, but Samantha took it a step further. He couldn't think of a single way that they could make that work. And that wasn't even due to the fact that the idea terrified him. Still, he knew she was right. They all knew it was their best option.

"But how?" he said without thinking.

"Do we even know where it's filmed?" Abagail asked.

They stopped talking again, all thinking the same thing. How had they not realized this before?

"We don't," Will said with a smirk. "But we know who does."

"Del!" Samantha yelled a bit too loudly, but her enthusiasm was matched by everyone else in the room.

"If we can convince him to help us, we could get in there!" Will agreed.

Samantha explained to Abagail and Jim that Del had moved from working in the room with Will to filming the videos for Servant Deena.

"That's perfect!" Abagail said.

"There's only one problem," Will reminded Samantha. "He doesn't even think of me as human."

"Well, then we show him that you are," Samantha said stubbornly, but Will thought back to the nineteen years where this man looked past him and didn't see even an ounce of humanity in his face when he accidently happened look at it.

"I don't know," he said hesitantly. "I really don't think he'll ever believe I'm a real person."

"Then let's show him that you are," Samantha said.

Abagail looked at Will for a moment and then cut in, "Can I just say how ridiculous it is that we actually have to be concerned that someone would not even realize you're a person? That's insane. It's like they look at someone else and see a person, and then they look at you and don't? That's appalling. You don't look any different from any of the Servants other than your legs, and same with Victoria. This is just crazy that we have to justify your mere humanity to people. I'm so sorry!"

"No," Will said. "You're right! Abagail! That's it! He doesn't see me as a person, but he sees everyone else as one. And I look just like everyone else from the middle up!"

"Yeah," she said. "That should be obvious!"

"But that's it! If we get him to think that I'm not me, then we can prove to him that I'm a person because of course he'd think I was, and then we can tell him it was me all along. He would never expect me to be out of that room. We just have to hide my legs and get him to have a conversation with me; then, once we're friends, we can reveal it and he'll understand!"

"Will! You're a genius!" Abagail exclaimed. "He'll never know and then once we show him, he'll have to understand!"

"Sounds great," Jim said, and then looked to his wife. "Do you think you can get him to come around for dinner or coffee or something, so he can meet Will?"

"Most definitely!" Samantha said. "I'll call him right now. I'll say I want to talk to him about the job or something. Do you think that'll work?"

"Don't see why not," Jim said. "I'd do it if someone asked me."

"Same here," Abagail said.

"Let's give it a try then!" Samantha smiled at them with confidence and pride in their new plan. "Who are you going to be though, Will? Like why will you be at our house?"

"We can say he's my boyfriend," Abagail suggested with a tiny smile that only Will saw.

"Makes sense to me," Will smiled slyly back at her.

"Sounds like a plan!" Samantha said getting up and grabbing her phone. "Let me go give him a call."

Samantha left quickly and Jim, Abagail, and Will sat there in silence waiting to hear what the verdict would be. Will questioned their plan in his mind, not wanting to admit any of the flaws he noticed in it, but still a bit concerned that Del wouldn't see him as human just as he hadn't all the years before. He tried to convince himself that this plan would work though, because it wouldn't be him that Del was seeing. It would be someone else. Someone who wasn't a creature.

Samantha returned within minutes trying to hold a straight face. They knew in a matter of seconds that he had said yes, though, because she couldn't contain her smile.

"He's coming tomorrow night for dinner!" she said cheerfully.

"Tomorrow?" Will asked surprised.

"Yes! Is that too soon?"

"No," Will lied, "It should be fine."

"You nervous?" Jim asked him.

"A bit," Will admitted. "It's just that for so many years he acted like I wasn't even there." Will started crying and Jim put his hand on his shoulder, "I just hope he'll see me tomorrow. I know that's what we need to do, I just don't know if I can take feeling so disregarded again."

"We'll be here with you this time," Jim said. "We'll make sure he sees you. I promise."

"Me too," Samantha and Abagail chorused at the same time.

Will took their word for it. He had trusted them this far and it had been fine. He was nervous that he knew this situation, this man, better though. But still, he saw their smiles and he knew regardless of what happened he'd be okay because he knew they'd protect him. He was soothed by that assurance for the rest of the night.

Chapter Ten

All of the Brokenness

The next day, Samantha, Abagail, and Jim raced home from their jobs as fast as they could, and along with Will, they spent the rest of the day preparing for dinner with Del. They had the kitchen make an enchilada dish and some rice and beans, and spent the afternoon cleaning the downstairs of the house so it would look nice for their company. After a few minutes of trying to figure out what they could do to hide Will's missing legs, they decided to cover the table with a floor length tablecloth and sit him on the opposite side of the place they had set for Del.

"What about when he gets here?" Will asked. "The polite thing to do would be to stand up and greet him, right? What should we do about that?"

"Oh you're right," Jim said. "I hadn't thought about that."

"We'll just get him to sit down really fast," Samantha said.

"That could work," Jim replied. "And Abagail and I can also be sitting already, so it'll be fine for y'all to just come and sit down with us all once you get the door."

"Yeah," Abagail said. "Let's do that."

None of them were really sure that would be a perfect solution, but it was the best idea they could come up with and they knew they had to come up with something soon.

Once they got the room set up, Abagail ran upstairs and grabbed some of her father's hair gel and helped Will make his hair look different enough that he would hopefully not be recognized earlier than intended.

Within minutes of finishing his hair, it was time for Del to arrive, so Abagail ran upstairs to put the gel away and they all got into their places. Abagail and Will sat together on one side of the table, Jim sat across from Abagail, and there was a place set for Del directly across from Will. Samantha was at the head of the table in between Will and where Del would be. They all sat staring at each other waiting for Del to arrive. Each of their hearts were beating faster than usual, and most of them were bouncing a bit in their chairs. No one said anything; they just waited in silence.

The doorbell rang, and they all jumped. For some reason it sounded just a bit louder and more jarring today than it ever had before. Will had to catch his breath. He was terrified to see Del again. He wasn't exactly sure what he would feel, but he *was* sure that it wasn't going to be comfortable knowing that Del was seeing him as human only because he wasn't really seeing *him* at all.

Samantha moved quickly to open the door, but not before looking at Will and her family and whispering, "We've got this y'all!"

They all smiled a bit, and watched Samantha make her way to the door.

"Hi, Servant Del!" she said as she swung the door open. "Good evening!"

"Good Evening, Servant Samantha," Del said kindly, but Samantha cringed. "Thank you for inviting me to dinner."

Will couldn't even see Del yet, but hearing his voice was interesting. He realized that in the room, he barely ever heard Del talk, but he still recognized the voice and felt a chill move down his spine.

"Of course!" Samantha smiled. "Thank you for coming! Why don't you come in? My family is already sitting down to eat."

Del followed her over to the table. She pulled out her chair and sat down. Del looked around to the rest of them before sitting.

"Hello," he said. "My name is Del." He extended his hand to Jim. Jim wasn't exactly sure what to do, so he stayed sitting, leaned forward and shook his hand. It was a little unnatural, but Del didn't seem to mind.

"Nice to meet you, Servant Del," Jim replied as they shook hands. "I'm Jim, Samantha's husband."

"Nice to meet you as well, Servant Jim," Del said, and turned to Abagail.

Before he could shake her hand though, Jim said, "Just Jim. Please don't say Servant."

"Oh," Del said. "Yes, now I remember. Sorry."

"It's fine," Abagail said, trying to lighten the mood and bring him back to introductions so it wouldn't be awkward. "I'm Abagail, Samantha's daughter!" She smiled and extended her hand, again still sitting. He reached out and shook it. Will could see in her eyes that she was fighting back anger, because she knew this was the man who had hurt her sister and him. She played it off well though, and he didn't notice.

Will then extended his hand, "I'm Will. Abagail's boyfriend." He spoke more shyly than he was hoping, but he gave him a firm handshake to make up for it.

"Well, nice to meet you both," Del said and then he finally sat down. Will was relieved, and he could tell that everyone else was too.

"So, Servant Del," Jim asked. "Do you like enchiladas?"

"Definitely," he replied politely.

"Then let's get started," Samantha said, and she grabbed the platter of enchiladas and scooped one onto her plate. She passed it to Del and he did the same.

"So, Ser... um... Samantha," Del asked. "How is the new job going?"

"Really well!" Samantha smiled. "I'm actually quite enjoying it."

"Oh really?" Del sounded surprised.

"Yes," Samantha said matter-of-factly, but then decided to change the subject so they didn't get ahead of themselves. "How is your new job?"

"I love it!" Del said. "Getting to serve Servant Deena is absolutely wonderful. Even just getting the chance to meet her was amazing, let alone getting to spend a bit of time with her every day."

"That's fantastic," Samantha said.

"Yeah," Del literally couldn't help but smiling. "It definitely makes up for having to spend the last twenty years with the creatures. I'm sure it will eventually be worth it for you, too."

"It already is," Samantha said, and Del really did not know what to do with that comment, so he just moved on.

"So what do y'all do?" he said, looking to the other people at the table.

Jim explained that he was a composter, who worked with a few other people to take everyone's composting bins and mix it all together, to help it biodegrade. He loved this job, because he felt that it was actually helping the Sovereignty and making it better, whereas he didn't think there were many other jobs these days that truly helped that. To Del, though, he just said he liked it. Del, again, was surprised, because neither of these jobs were looked at as a positive assignment.

Abagail then told him that she was a grade one teacher and that she absolutely loved it. It was wonderful for her to get to work with all of the children, and she hoped that this too was a job where she could actually make a difference. The fact that the three of them all had jobs that they liked was a rare occurrence, but it worked out well for them because they all asked for the jobs that no one else wanted. They were the ones that took real work, where they actually had to serve.

"So," Del said, and looked directly into Will's eyes for the first time ever. "What do you do, then?"

Will froze. It took a second for him to come up with something and be bold enough to talk directly to Del. He thought briefly about all the times he and Jaden had wished that they could get him to talk to them, and now that he was, it was exciting and terrifying. Will was quick enough to reply, though, that no one noticed anything. He was impressed with himself for speaking up, and for coming up with a lie in time.

"I actually just started a new job too," he explained. "I'm one of the new guards for the... um... creatures." He had never called them that before. He had never called them people either, though, just 'the others'. It was weird to use the term he so deeply hated.

"Oh..." Del said, surprised. "I can't believe I never saw you in there."

"I just started working the same day as Samantha so I think we only really saw each other in passing."

"Really?" Del was surprised. "I'm sorry I don't recognize you, then. I would've thought I would see you there, but I guess I was just so ready to get out of there I wasn't paying attention to all the people."

"Yeah, that's probably why you didn't see me," Will said, and three of the people in the room had to hold back laughter because of his sarcasm, but Del didn't pick up on it.

"I'm just so glad I finally got out of that job," Del said, relieved. "Kudos to you, Samantha, for seeming okay with it."

"Not just seeming," she said quietly, and then spoke up a bit. "I'm so glad you're liking your new job with Servant Deena though. Tell me more about that."

They listened to Del go on for a while about how wonderful the job was, and more importantly, how wonderful Servant Deena was. They couldn't stand listening to all of the ways that he was praising her after seeing what she was doing to people like Will and Victoria, but they knew they had to listen to it so that they could eventually get his help.

"So, Will," he finally asked. "Do you like working as a guard? I assume it would be a pretty easy job, saying as the only creature you really had to worry about, I took care of years ago."

They all cringed. Will didn't want to respond for Victoria's sake and for the sake of her family sitting around him. He knew he had to though.

"It's not too bad," was all Will could muster.

"Yeah, I guess," Del said. "It's just kind of a bad vibe in there and all, being so close to all the creatures."

"Kind of," Will answered, and then he figured, getting a bit bolder, he'd pose a question of his own. "What was it like for you working in the room with all of them for all those years?"

"Oh," Del started. "It was horrifying. All of the brokenness. All of the imperfections. I could hardly stand to look at them."

"Sometimes I hear them making noises and saying things." Will went on with his game, "Did that bother you?"

"Definitely," he said. "I mean at first, part of me thought that I should respond, but the man training me, just like I trained you, Samantha, told me that if I did that it would lead to really big issues. He never really specified what they were I guess, but I didn't want to find out."

"That's so interesting," Abagail started playing along. "What kind of issues do you think it would have led to? I mean you'd been in there so many years, you have to have some idea of what he was talking about by now, right?"

"Honestly, no," Del said. "I really don't have any clue what he was talking about. I mean I had to deal with quite a few issues, but really I just tried to get in and out as fast as I could to avoid any problems that could have come up. That's probably your best bet too, Samantha."

"You're probably right," Samantha said. "But it's just so hard not to respond to them."

"Yeah. It was for me too at first," Del explained. "But you've just got to look past them. Just keep telling yourself, they're just creatures. Every time you want to respond, remind yourself... just creat ures."

"Are they, though?" Abagail asked. Will, Jim, and Samantha jumped a bit, hoping her question wasn't too soon.

"Well yeah," Del said. "Of course they are. That's why they're in there."

"Really?" Abagail continued. "Why are they creatures?"

"Because they have imperfections," Del explained, like it was the most clear idea in the world.

"But like, why does that make them not people?" Abagail kept going. Everyone else just sat silently, hoping she knew what she was doing.

"Well because they can't reach perfection. God is perfect, and we, people, are made in God's image, so that means we need to strive to be like God and be as perfect as we can be. They can't be perfect because they have an imperfection."

"Why do they have imperfections?" Del seemed generally interested in the conversation so Abagail knew it was okay to continue.

"Because there's something wrong with them."

"Why is it wrong?"

"Because it's not... right..." Del didn't know what to say, finally he just said, "Well, they smell bad. And they make weird noises."

"Do you think they'd do those things if they weren't in that room?" Abagail continued in a curious and non confrontational way.

"I'm not sure..."

"What if someone taught them how to wash themselves? Then they wouldn't smell. And what if their weird noises are just them trying to talk but no one helped teach them? Could that maybe be true?"

"I guess so..."

"So then is it wrong? Or are *we* wrong for not teaching them?"

Samantha cut in at this point, "Are they imperfect, or just different? And if there are people who can't see, if they can get around just fine using their other senses somehow, does that mean they're less perfect or just different? And same with people who can't walk. If they get around using another method? Or people who can't talk, but communicate through body language or visual cues, is that imperfect, or is it just different?"

Del was stunned. "But we call them creatures." He went back to the facts. "There has to be a reason we do."

"People used to say that people who had different skin tones were creatures, and that one of the genders was imperfect. Don't you remember learning that in school?"

"Yeah," Del said thoughtfully.

"So, could this be like that?" Will asked this time. "Could those that the Sovereignty calls creatures really be just as much people as us?"

"No," Del said, but couldn't continue.

"But you're different from Abagail, right, and Jim or Samantha. But one of them isn't better or worse than you, right?"

"Yeah."

"So then," Will continued, "Why do you think that someone who is different than you in those ways is so much less than you?"

"Because that's what they told me to think," Del admitted.

"Is that what you want to think?" Jim questioned.

"I don't know," Del said. "I guess I don't think so. Not anymore."

"Those people who you looked past, Del," Samantha explained. "They're people."

Del sat in silence for a moment, just thinking, and then said, "I think the man before me was wrong. I think there was a creature... a man... in there who could talk just like we could. I wish I had responded to him. I felt guilty for not responding for the first few days, and then I just had to block it out because I felt so badly. And all the creatures... people... in there who tried to get me to touch them... people deserve to be touched. I didn't do that. I should have done that."

"Someone did, though, Del," Samantha assured him.

"That man you're talking about," Will smiled. "Did he say something like, 'excuse me Servant, but what is the date? And is Servant Deena still in power? And do you know what happened to Grace Josephs?'."

"Yeah, Will," Del was surprised. "That's exactly what he said. I should have replied, shouldn't I? The man before me told me he was just making stuff up. That he was just repeating things he had heard in the past. But he wasn't, was he? I knew he wasn't. I just knew it. I should have replied. They're... people! And I treated them like creatures."

"He wasn't just repeating things," Will said. "But it's okay, you didn't know. That's what the Sovereignty told you to think, but now that you know differently, I think you should respond to him."

"How?" Del asked. "Can I sneak in with you, Samantha, so I can apologize to him? To all of them."

"You don't need to," Samantha smiled.

"You can tell him right now," Will said and he pulled himself down off of his chair. His head was about level with the table, so he could barely see the increasingly confused look on Del's face. He quickly made his way around the side of the table, past Samantha's chair, and when he emerged on the other side of it, Del could see him fully.

"Will?" Del asked, incredibly shocked.

"Will Josephs." Will extended his hand. "It's nice to finally get to meet you, as myself, after all these years."

Del took his hand but barely shook it. He just sat there in his chair, holding Will's hand, and he started to sob.

"I'm so sorry, Will," he choked through tears. "I am so incredibly sorry. I knew you weren't just a parrot. I knew it and I shouldn't have listened to them saying you were. I should have known, Will. I'm so sorry."

"It's okay," Will said, taking Del's hand and holding it in between both of his. "The Sovereignty tells us we have to believe what they do. It's not your fault for falling for their lie. But Del, I'm not a creature. And neither are any of the others in that room." He paused realizing he too had never regarded himself or the others as people either. "Neither are any of those people. Those people are just that. They're people. And they're my friends."

Del continued crying, "You are most definitely not a creature, Will. You're a person. Just like any of us in this room. I can't believe my ignorance. My apathy. That I would ever think differently. I'm so sorry."

"It's not just you, though," Samantha cut in. "It's everyone. There isn't a person in this Sovereignty, except us in this room, and maybe a few other parents of people with 'imperfections' that understand that. But that's the issue. It isn't an imperfection in Will or in any of the other people in there. It's an imperfection in the Sovereignty."

"Oh my gosh," Del said. "You're right. You are so right. We spend all these years hearing how perfect the Sovereignty is and how if we can only be more perfect, we will be good enough. But it's really an imperfection in the Sovereignty, not in the people. That's insane."

"Isn't it?" Will asked rhetorically.

"I cannot believe this," Del said. He sat there looking at Will in absolute astonishment. "I just had a whole dinner with you, thinking you were someone who you weren't and knowing you were a person, but had I seen you before I sat down, I would never have believed that. But it's true. The Sovereignty is wrong."

Suddenly Del dropped Will's hand. "What did I do?" he cried again. "I hurt that girl. I broke her legs," Del was shaking. "And I didn't even feel anything but relief that I didn't have to go near her again. I hurt her so badly. She is a person."

Samantha, Jim, Abagail, and Will all looked at each other.

Finally Samantha broke the news, "She is a person, Del. And not just any person. She is my daughter."

"And my daughter," Jim laughed.

"And my little sister," Abagail explained.

"And my friend," Will added with a sad smile at all of them.

"Oh no," Del whispered. "No! No! No! No! No!" He continued to get louder. "Oh no! Please forgive me. I can't believe it. I can't believe I did that. I can't believe I didn't know. I am so, so sorry." He put his hand up to his mouth, looked down at his lap, not wanting to look any of them in the eye, and sobbed.

Samantha stood up and came over towards them. "It's okay," she said. "You understand what you did now. Don't beat yourself up. The Sovereignty convinced you it was the right thing to do, but you know it's not now, and that's what counts, because now you can do something about it."

"What can I do?" Del said. "Your daughter can't walk, now, and she probably will never be able to, all because of me. I can't do anything to help that. I've already screwed it up too badly."

"You can." Jim said.

"Honestly, who cares if she can't walk if she's strapped to a chair her whole life," Samantha said blatantly. "That's the problem. We need to get them out of that room and into the Sovereignty."

"That's why we invited you tonight, Del." Will explained.

"You can help us," Abagail said.

"I can?" Del asked. "How are you going to do that?"

Will, Samantha, Abagail, and Jim explained everything to Del. They started with Will and what it was like in the room and what he did to make it better. Del was amazed and awestruck that that was all going on while he was in there and he never knew. Will told him about all the other people and what they were like and Del remembered more and more things that continued to convince him that they were in fact people. Finally, they explained how they got Will out, what was happening now, and how they thought they could make a change.

"You want to get on that screen?" Del asked.

"That's the only way they're going to listen to me." Will said.

"You're right," Del admitted. "Then that's what we've got to do. I think I can make it happen."

"Good!" Samantha said.

"What do we need to do?" Jim asked.

Del hesitated for a second, sitting there thinking about how they could do this seemingly impossible thing. "Well, the first thing you should know is where the building is that we film in. That will have a lot to do with what we need."

For this reason alone, the Servants were not allowed to know where Servant Deena was, when she filmed these videos. Del explained that every day they used a green screen so that it would appear that she was moving around the Sovereignty, when in reality, they were just standing in a single room that is hidden underground. Because he worked for her now, Del had to be there so he had to know where it was. He shared with them that it was really out in the middle of one of the forests adjacent to the Sovereignty.

"Do you think we can break into it?" Samantha asked boldly.

"Maybe. Here's the biggest problem. The only entrance is through the roof and the rest of the building is underground, so you have to climb down in. Servant Deena and Servant Michael before her had it set that way so that it was harder to get into. It barely looks like a room at all because it's hidden so well. I can get you there, but I'm not exactly sure how we're going to get you in. Servant Deena is the only one who knows how to unlock the door."

"Oh," Will smiled. "Unlocking things is definitely not a problem." He looked up at Samantha and they all laughed. They told Del all about Victoria and her innate ability to unlock everything. Del remembered quite well, and quite sadly.

"Do you think you can get her out, Samantha?" Jim asked.

"Yeah," she said with confidence. "When I helped Will escape, there was no reason we couldn't have just walked out. No one would have known. I can just wait until the guards leave and then I'll just push her chair out and get her in my car. I can watch her today and see how she unlocks Jaden and hopefully then I can do that by myself every day, unless I don't need to because of what happens out here."

She let out a big breath. The idea of having her daughter home was almost too good to be true. She saw Jim and Abagail's excitement build, too.

"That truly is our best bet," Jim smiled, and Will looked to Abagail thinking she was going to say something, but she was far too excited to speak. A few tears rolled down her face, and Will put his hand on her knee. She smiled and wiped the tears away.

"Let's do it!" Will said, almost as excited as the rest of them.

"Okay, so if we can get y'all in," Del thought aloud. "Then I don't think the rest will be too challenging. I'll be standing there with the camera, so I'll focus it on Will, and the rest of y'all will have to keep Servant Deena away. Then I think we've got it!"

"Sounds easy enough!" Samantha exclaimed.

"Yeah," Jim added, "We're really gonna do this!"

"Yeah we are!" Abagail and Will said at the same time.

The excitement in the room was building so quickly that none of them could completely stay still.

Suddenly, Del looked at the time.

"We've only got about an hour until the message tonight," Del said disappointedly. "So I need to head out and get to work. Would one of you want to come with me just to see where it is, and then come back before it starts so you can be counted?"

"Yeah," Jim said. "I'll go."

"Okay, sounds good," Del said.

Jim and Del grabbed their coats and started out the door.

"I'll be back soon," Del told Samantha, Will, and Abagail. "I think it's important that we do this in the next few days."

"I agree," Samantha said. "I'll try to get Victoria here as soon as I can, and we'll start working out what Will wants to say."

"Sounds like a plan," Del smiled. He gave them all hugs, and as he reached out to hug Will he whispered, "I'm so sorry, Will."

"It's okay," Will said, and it was. "Thank you for helping."

"It's seriously the least I could do."

After that, Jim and Del left and shut the door behind them. Will, Samantha, and Abagail were all standing there in between the kitchen and living room. As the door shut, Samantha turned to look at Abagail and Will.

"Oh my goodness!" Samantha said and literally jumped up and down a few times. "That went so well!"

"It did!" Will said, just as excitedly.

Samantha ran over and gave both her daughter and Will big hugs. The excitement radiated off of her. As she let go of Abagail, Abagail turned to Will and gave him a hug. In their excitement, they didn't think about the fact that Samantha was standing right there, and they leaned in for their second kiss. As they finished kissing, Abagail and Will looked up to see a very shocked Samantha standing in front of them. They paused.

"Oh." Samantha looked quizzically at each of them. "When did this happen?"

"A few nights ago," Abagail told her mom excitedly.

Samantha gave them a brief puzzled look, and then decided to continue their conversation about how incredibly well the night with Del went. After about half an hour, Jim returned, and eventually they watched Servant Deena for the last time that day. The excitement of the night continued for a few more hours, and then they all made their way upstairs to go to bed.

Chapter Eleven

Fear that went Unsaid

Will was able to fall asleep quickly after all of the excitement that night. He dreamed of his life before entering the room, all of the people he met while he was inside, and what his life was now like on the outside. Around four a.m. he woke up and knew that he would not easily be able to go back to sleep. Lying there for a minute, he thought about the last few days and his heart was warm with the love and acceptance he felt. It amazed him that this all happened so suddenly. It was still so surreal to him that he was here, as he looked around the room to see the dresser, closet, and other typical bedroom belongings. He should still be in the room with Jaden, Victoria, and everyone else. The fact that he was here now, was astonishing. He knew that it was only due to Samantha's willingness to take a chance on him, and possibly a small bit of his own bravery along with Victoria's and Jaden's willingness to help. Knowing that all of those people had made it possible for him to be here was such an honor to him. He knew that now he needed to do all he could to keep the courage to continue to fight for Jaden and Victoria, and for everyone else in the room in the same way that they were fighting for him there. He couldn't wait to figure out more of the plan with Abagail, Jim, Samantha, and Del, and he was also so incredibly excited to get to see Victoria again. He could only imagine the excitement of her family about it as well.

After lying there for a few minutes with a smile on his face, he decided that he would head downstairs and get a cup of tea. He got up as quietly as he could, but as he made his way to the stairs, he heard voices whispering intensely below him. He paused for a second to let his eyes adjust to the darkness as he tried to make out who it was.

As he moved close enough to hear their voices, he realized that Abagail and Samantha were both already downstairs sitting on the couch sipping tea. They couldn't see Will from where he was standing on the stairs, but he could see the tops of their heads. He stood quietly, not wanting to interrupt what they were saying.

"You know I'd do anything for him, Abagail," Will could barely make out Samantha's words. "I just don't think it's a good idea."

"It's not up to you, Mom," Abagail said with both strength and gentleness. "I really love him."

Will froze. Was she talking about him? Or another man? He figured it had to be someone else. He was hurt, but it was what he had expected to happen at some point. He definitely had feelings for Abagail, but he knew she could do better.

"Abagail," Samantha continued, "You don't know what it will be like."

"I do, mom," Abagail retorted. "You seem to forget that Victoria is my sister."

"But you were so young. You don't remember the comments, or the terrible things people did, or what it was like when they took her away."

"Yes, I do. I remember when Angela came by and found out we still had Victoria. You thought I was too young to understand, but I heard her say how worthless she was, I heard her say she didn't deserve to be here or to be alive and that we were better off just killing her. I remember that, and I remember right after that moment running up to Victoria's room, holding her in my six-year-old arms, and promising her that I would never let anything bad happen to her and that I would fight all the people who said mean things. I remember a few years later when all of the people Dad worked with came over and Victoria got out and you and Dad spent weeks and weeks convincing them not to say anything, paying them off even, just so that you could keep your daughter, but what you don't know is that I helped convince them too. I saw them when they dropped their kids off at school in fifth grade, and I told them that if they did anything to my sister I would make their children's lives a living hell. And don't think for a second I don't remember later that day when Victoria got out of the house and the Servants found her and grabbed her. I remember her screaming. I remember running towards her with you and Dad and I remember the Servants pulling us back. I remember the way they grabbed her and carried her as if she didn't mean anything at all to them, as if she was just a heap of trash. I remember thinking that I would never see my sister again, but I also remember that day vowing to keep fighting for her day in and day out, just like you and Dad.

"And I remember the other times too, Mom. The good times. I remember our sleepovers in each other's rooms. I remember painting her nails. I remember telling her all my secrets and how she knew things that no one else knew about me and I knew things that no one else knew about her. I remember the way that she used to laugh every time she got something unlocked and I would laugh with her because I knew she was so much smarter than everyone else. Trust me Mom, I know it's hard. But I also know it's so, so good." Abagail finished talking, and Samantha stared at her for a second.

"I'm so glad that you and your sister have such a strong bond, Abagail, of course I am, but getting yourself into this relationship is dangerous. I just want what's best for you, and I can tell you, this is going to lead to a ton of pain. People are going to hate you for it. They might even try to kill you. And that's only if this whole thing works out anyway."

"It will," Abagail insisted. "And *we* will. It wasn't just a one time thing. I promise. I understand what life would be like with him, and he understand what life was like for me more than anyone else ever will. I love him, Mom, and I'm sorry, but there isn't anything you can do about that."

"It's just going to be so hard on you," Samantha said. "That's all I'm worried about."

"Then why did you bring him here?"

Will was shaking. They were talking about him. There was no doubting that now, and he stood there, unable to move, wanting to run upstairs and back to bed and pretend that he had never heard any of this, or out the door and somewhere far away. But he didn't have anywhere to go. Samantha had brought him here. That's all he had. He stared at them as they continued to talk. Tears streamed down his face.

"Abagail, that's not fair," Samantha argued. "You know why I brought him here."

"Why, Mom?" she asked. "Maybe I don't. I thought you brought him here so that you could help give him and everyone else in that room a good life. But now I think you just brought him here to get Victoria back."

"Of course I didn't," Samantha said calmly. "I love Will. I love him like a son. I would do anything for him, or Jaden, or Victoria."

"But you wouldn't let him be part of your family?"

"He is as much a part of our family as he needs to be," Samantha answered. "I brought him here to help give him, and all of them, the life they deserve."

"Well, the life he deserves is a life with someone who loves him and understands him and someone who he loves and understands as well. Why can't I be that person? Why can't he be that person for me?"

"Because I don't want you to have a life of fighting for people to believe you're worthy. I don't want anyone to have that life, but it is a reality for Will and Victoria and it doesn't need to be a reality for you. I love you, and I don't want you to have to struggle to stand up for him your whole life."

"Do you love him?"

"Yes," Samantha smiled slightly. "I love him very, very much. You know that."

"Then why don't you want him to be happy?"

"That's not fair, Abagail. You know that's exactly what I want. I just don't want his happiness to be at the expense of your happiness."

Will could almost feel his heart fall at that. He didn't want his happiness to diminish hers either, but to hear Samantha say those words broke him. She had quite literally been his savior, and knowing that she thought that about him hurt. It hurt in a place so deep that it had never been reached in the years he spent being tortured by the Servants.

"Mom, it wouldn't be."

"Yes," Samantha said. "Yes, it would. Don't be naive, Abagail, you know it would be a life of advocating for him and fighting for him and possibly even getting hurt for him."

"And you're willing to do that for Victoria, right?"

"Of course," Samantha said.

"I thought you were willing to do that for Will, too."

"I am."

"Then why can't I?"

"Because I don't want to see you in that kind of pain."

"I won't be. The good will outweigh any of that, Mom. I can't believe you went through all the work of bringing him here, but don't want him to get married and have a normal life."

"I do," Samantha said. "You know I do. Just..."

"Just what?" Abagail cut in at her pause. "Just what, Mom?"

"Just not with you."

Will took a deep breath. He could barely breathe listening to them. It hurt him so badly.

"That's not fair," Abagail countered.

"Well it's not fair for you to have to take that on."

"No, Mom, you're right, it's not," Abagail said sarcastically, getting angry now. "It's not fair that I would get to have a husband that understands exactly what it is I went through in losing my little sister. It's not fair I would get a husband who spent years learning what it means to really love people. It's not fair that I would get a husband who fit in so well with my family that he felt like he was always part of it. It's not fair that I would get a husband who knows what pain is like and knows how to overcome what seems like the impossible. It's really not fair to everyone else. I feel bad for everyone who wouldn't be as lucky as I would be."

"Abagail," Samantha said and stared at her, not saying anymore.

"What, Mom?" Abagail asked, clearly upset.

"Love, I just don't want you to be in pain."

"I've been in pain before, Mom, and I'll be in pain again. With Will, I'll just have someone to share it with. You risked so much taking him out of that room. You risked putting yourself in pain to love him. Why can't I?"

"Because it's going to be so much," Samantha whispered. "You'll never stop."

"And I'm okay with that. He would do it for me. He did it for everyone in that room for so many years."

"Yeah, but he won't need to do it for you. You'll need to do it for him. And that's not fair..."

"Why is it not fair, Mom?" Abagail asked pointedly.

"Because it's not... equal," Samantha said defeatedly, knowing what she had just done.

"*What's* not equal?"

"Abagail!" Samantha stopped.

"No, Mom," Abagail pushed on. "*What's* not equal?"

"You and Will, but you know I don't mean it like *that*," Samantha defended herself.

"Like what, Mom? Because right now," Abagail threw her arms in the air. "Right now, you sound just like the Servants." She stood up and whipped around to leave. She started rushing towards the stairs with tears streaming down her face. Will didn't have time to move.

"Abagail!" Samantha yelled.

"Abagail," Will whispered and she saw him standing just a few feet away, halfway down the stairs, with tears streaming down his face as well.

Abagail stopped in her tracks and stared, "Will."

Samantha turned to see what had happened and saw the two of them standing there. She heard her daughter's voice whisper his name and she knew what she had just done. Nothing could take it back now.

Samantha's eyes met Will's. They all stood there for what seemed like an eternity. Will struggled to get his breath. All the love he had felt over the last few days disappeared in an instant, and he felt unwelcome and unwanted in this house and in this room right now. He wanted to run, but there was nowhere to run to. He stood there looking up at her, unable to speak.

"Will," Samantha finally whispered.

"No," Will said quietly shaking his head.

"Will," Samantha repeated sadly.

Abagail put her hand on Will's shoulder and looked up at her mom, too. Will let her leave it there for a moment, and then he brushed it off. He was hurting so badly from Samantha's words, but he also knew she was right. They weren't equal and it would be harder on Abagail if he was in her life. Samantha was the only person who had believed in his equality enough to do something about it, and to now hear that she really didn't believe in it at all felt like more than he could hold. It broke him knowing that she didn't really think of him as equal, even though he knew her point to be true. He should have known it was too good to be true. He shouldn't have agreed to come out with her. He should have just stayed in the room. He didn't want to cause any extra pain to her or Abagail or anyone for that matter. But she was the one who told him he wouldn't, and now she was telling her daughter that he would.

"Will," Samantha whispered, now crying too. "I'm so sorry. I didn't mean it. I swear. I didn't mean it like that."

"But you said it," Will mustered up the voice to remind her. He looked up at Abagail but could barely meet her eyes because of the shame he felt in his heart. He really did love her, but it was stupid for him to want that. It would be so hard on her. As his eyes moved from hers, he let them fall. He told himself that this was the last time he could look at her with love. Otherwise, it wouldn't be fair.

"Will," Samantha whispered again, at a deep loss for words.

Will absolutely could not look her in the eye. She had betrayed him. She had lied to him about what she thought of him and who she thought he was. More than feeling angry, he was sad. He was broken, because he no longer felt loved. Suddenly, he thought of his mother's words, what he would whisper to himself when he was feeling unloved in the room, but now they seemed to hold no weight. Now, the person who had wanted to prove to him that they were true was acting as though they were nothing but a kindness made up to make him feel better about himself. He couldn't look at her, because if he did, he felt like he would melt.

He turned away. Abagail reached out her hand, but didn't touch him, even though he was close enough to her that she could have. She clearly wasn't sure what to do. Will started making his way back up the stairs. In all of his time here, he had found it so exciting or just commonplace that he was able to get himself up the stairs by holding onto the banister and the wall and pulling himself up. Now, as he did it, he let the tears flow down his face, knowing that no one else had to do it this way. He felt more broken by the loss of his legs now than he ever had before, and all he wanted was to disappear.

The closest thing that he could do to disappearing was to hide back in Victoria's room. When he made his way in, he noticed all the thing that he had looked at with such awe and excitement only minutes before. Now they all seemed to feel heavy, as if he were burdening them too. He tried not to think about it as he made his way to the bed. He could barely see what was going on because it was so dark and his tears were blocking most of his field of vision. He could hear Samantha and Abagail following quietly behind him, but he tried not to care. He tried to ignore their footsteps and their soft tears and deep breaths.

He sat down on Victoria's bed and looked to the doorway. The two of them were standing there, staring at him. No one knew what to do. There was so much pain in Will's heart that Samantha and Abagail could feel it, too. They hurt for each other, but that didn't matter anymore because Samantha's words had put a divide up between them all. Will knew that her words were out of love for her daughter and hope that she would have a good life, but somehow, thinking about what she had said made it even worse. If he thought she had just lied and didn't care at all, it would be easier, but knowing that she *did* love him, but didn't love him enough to want him in her daughter's life felt even more saddening.

Samantha slowly made her way into the room and Abagail followed behind her. Neither of them had any words to say, they just wanted Will to know they were there. Normally their presence would have been his greatest comfort, but right now, it did nothing but make him feel more alone. His tears continued and he wasn't sure if this pain would ever go away. He tried all he could to make himself stop crying, so that they would leave, but even as the tears slowed down, the pain was obvious in his eyes. He didn't know how long they had been standing there, but it felt like it had been hours of them all just staring at each other. He felt, even that this was a burden to them. Having to stand here and make sure he was okay was yet another thing that they had to do to help him, and now he knew that wasn't really what they wanted, or at least not what was best for them. He felt like he was taking up their time even now, and he wanted that feeling to stop, so he did the only thing he could think of to try to get them to leave.

"So," he said, wiping his tears. "You're still going to get Victoria tomorrow, right?"

Samantha took a deep breath and then said, "Yes," with a more defeated tone than Will had ever heard her use. It hurt him to know that even that was because of him. Now suddenly everything was reminding him of just how much of a burden he was.

"Then you should probably get some sleep," he said, hoping that this would at least make them leave.

"Will," Samantha breathed and started walking over to him.

"No," Will said and she stopped. "Just go."

"Will," Abagail broke in.

"You too," Will said poignantly. "Your mom's right. I am too much for you to take on. I'm just a burden for you, Abagail, I could never be anything more than that."

"Will, you know that's not true!" Abagail insisted.

"You know it *is*," Will replied.

"I don't think of you as a burden; I would never think of you as a burden," Abagail continued. "You heard me tell my mom all the reasons why I would be lucky to be with you."

"But I would still be a burden, Abagail. That's just a fact. Because I have an imperfection, or at least because people say that I do, I will always be an extra weight, an extra fight, for anyone I'm close to. It's not your fault; It's just my imperfection."

"No it's not, Will," Samantha said. "You know that's not what I was saying."

"But it's true, isn't it?" Will commented. "That's why you were saying it. It doesn't matter if you believe I have an imperfection, the other Servants do, and that's enough to make me a liability for you and your family."

"Will, you are not a liability. You are not a burden," Samantha attempted to console him.

"You said I was," Will reminded her.

"But... Will," Samantha continued. "You know what I meant."

"Yes, and I also know what the other Servants mean and what that would mean if you were to spend a life with me."

"Will," Samantha said. "We would be lucky to spend a life with you."

"No, you wouldn't," Will started crying again. "You're just lying now. You said exactly the opposite of that just a few minutes ago. You said it wouldn't be fair for you to have to spend a life with me."

"I was scared," Samantha admitted. "I'm so sorry, Will."

"Don't be sorry about that," Will said, raising his voice. "You were right. Be sorry that you tried to convince me otherwise. That was where you went wrong."

"Will," Samantha was crying now, too.

"Just go to bed, Samantha," Will told her. "You have to go get Victoria in the morning."

Abagail and Samantha looked at him, and all he wanted was for them to leave. He couldn't stop the feeling of brokenness that he had right now, and having them standing there was only making it worse. Suddenly he knew what he needed to do to make them leave.

"Goodnight, Servant Samantha, goodnight Servant Abagail," he said angrily.

"Will!" Abagail said fiercely.

"You said it yourself, *Servant* Abagail," Will reminded her. "Your mom is just as bad as the Servants."

"But Will," she continued, but Will cut her off.

"Goodnight Servants. I'll see you in the morning so we can finish our plan so I can get out of your hair. Then you won't have to deal with me anymore."

"That's not what we want," Samantha said.

"Goodnight Servants," Will repeated.

"Goodnight Will," Abagail whispered with sadness and love in her voice, knowing that they were not going to make any progress tonight.

"I'm sorry," Samantha whispered. They stared at each other for a few moments longer, and then Abagail started to make her way out and Samantha followed slowly. Will watched them disappear out the door and he heard them make their way into their respective rooms without a word to each other.

He felt the hot tears continue to stream down his cheeks. His eyes hurt from crying so much and his chest hurt maybe from the same thing, or maybe simply from the feeling of worthlessness that took over his heart. He laid there and didn't get a moment more of sleep for the rest of the night. He didn't really think about anything either. He just held onto the pain of abandonment that the Sovereignty had so easily made his reality as he waited out the last few hours of the night.

Chapter Twelve

Home Again

Will reluctantly made his way downstairs in the morning. It took a lot of self-convincing to leave Victoria's room. He knew deep in his heart that even if he was a burden on Samantha, Abagail, and Jim, that he still needed to fight so that the Servants wouldn't see the others as a burden anymore. He doubted that would happen now, but if Samantha was still willing to try, even for Victoria's sake, he figured he would go along with it. He owed it to them for helping him get out, even though he wished, for the first time in his life, that he was back in the room.

He was the last one downstairs that morning, and he quickly realized that they had explained to Jim what had happened. Abagail was clearly not happy with her mother, and Jim seemed like he really just did not know what to do. Today was supposed to be an exciting day. Victoria was going to come back and Abagail and Jim were going to get to see her for the first time in years. But instead of the joy that they had going to bed the night before, they sat around the table eating breakfast in silence.

Will felt guilty that he was the source of the awkwardness, so he finally attempted to take at least that burden off of his hosts.

"You really are getting Victoria today, right Samantha?" he asked. He was trying to make conversation, figure out his personal plan, and make up for calling her a Servant last night. He still came across as rather cold, but Samantha played along.

"Yes," Samantha said. "Of course I am. Are you still planning to get on camera?"

"I don't see why not," Will said, although he did. He could think of a million reasons why it was a bad idea, including the fact that he was just utterly terrified at the fact that he would be speaking to so many people without feeling an ounce of worth.

"Okay," Samantha said very politely. "Then the plan is still in motion?"

"As far as I'm concerned," Will matched her tone. It was so uncomfortable to go from such a space of love and acceptance and excitement last night, to a formal, planning tone today. But this was where they were now and if they wanted to move forward, then this is what they would have to do. It hurt them all deeply, knowing that was the only thing holding them together, but none of them mentioned it, afraid it would make them unravel in a way they could not repair.

They ate the rest of their breakfast in silence and after what seemed like a long time, the broadcast finally came on, and Servant Deena spoke to everyone just as chipper as she always was. For some reason, her fake joy made everything even more uncomfortable, if that was possible. Will didn't know what to do, but he knew that soon, he was going to be the one up there, if everything worked the way they were hoping it would. That scared him, but also gave him the slightest bit of hope.

Samantha glanced at Will when the time came for the pledge. She stood and put her hand over her heart as they were forced to do each time, but she, like her daughter and husband did not speak just as they normally do. Will saw her staring and took her glance to mean, "See, I'm not as bad as the Servants. You know I'm not."

Will wasn't sure what he knew at this point. He still thought he knew that she loved him, but he also knew she didn't want him. He wondered, can she not want something that she loves? He wasn't sure. He didn't really want to find out. He just met her gaze with an understanding look, but still with pain seen deeply in his eyes. Samantha knew she had hurt him, but wasn't sure what to do, and wasn't ready to do anything for fear that it would make it worse.

As the message came to an end and the screen went black, Will stood up and the four of them moved back over into the kitchen, still somberly.

"How are we going to do this?" Jim finally asked.

"Do what?" Samantha questioned.

"Well, it's going to be hard for you to get Victoria out on your own, right?" Jim said. "But Abagail and I need to go to our jobs so no one notices anything weird happening if we're not accounted for."

"I'm sure I can manage by myself," Samantha thought for a second.

"Mom," Abagail interjected, "I don't know. You're going to have to push her and her chair out of there all by yourself. You really think you can do it?"

"Probably," Samantha said with a bit of skepticism.

"Really?" Abagail continued, clearly still bitter after last night. "Because if you get stuck half way, then we're all screwed."

"Well then what do you want me to do?" Samantha snapped.

"Take me with you," Will said blatantly. "I don't have to be at a job, and I already have a way of carrying Victoria that works for us, so all you'll have to do is get her to the loading room and then I can get her from there."

"You're right," Samantha said. "But you'll have to hide in the bottom of the car until the Servants leave. It'll be a couple hours."

"That's fine," Will said.

"Okay. Sounds like a plan then," Samantha stood up to grab her bag. She had the car pull around to the front of the house so that Will could hop in without anyone seeing. Abagail and Jim were on lookout and got him safely in.

"Good luck," Abagail said, trying to sound excited.

"You've got this," Jim added.

Abagail gave Will a brief look of kindness, and Will pulled his eyes away quickly. He knew that even if this plan worked, that Samantha was right, they shouldn't be together. He just wanted to get this part of the plan over with so that he could move on and somehow find a new life for himself where he wasn't a burden on anyone. Matching Abagail's kind look would only play into their fantasy that a relationship was a good idea.

He watched her and her father walk away, and then was left alone in the car with Samantha. He looked down at his lap quietly, wishing that he could be anywhere but where he was. There wasn't anything either of them could say right now that would make this less awkward, so they drove in silence for a while. Will fiddled with the shirt he was wearing, which belonged to Jim. He still wasn't used to wearing a real shirt after wearing his gown for so many years.

As they got closer to the building, Samantha turned to Will. He looked back at her shyly for a second before looking down. He still couldn't look her in the eye without thinking about the burden that he was to her that she had so blatantly put words to last night. He let her speak though, without really looking at her.

"Do you want to come in with me? I know you'll come in at the end just to the loading room to help us get out, but if you want to come into the room with everyone else, you can. I don't really know how we'd do it, but if you want to go in and see everyone, we will make it happen," Samantha told him.

"No, I can't," Will said quietly.

"You can. I'll help you get in and out without them seeing you," Samantha kindly added. "And don't choose not to just because you're upset with me. If you want to go in, I've got you, I promise."

"No, it's not that," Will said. "I really can't. Like emotionally. I know that I'm out here and all the others are still in there, but if I go and see them that will only make it real and it will be too hard for me to leave.

I'd feel too guilty again and I'd miss them all again, too."

"Makes sense," Samantha said, and Will cut her off.

"And also, I'm not upset with you, Samantha. I'm upset with myself. I'm upset that there isn't anything I can do to make it so that I'm not a burden on you and your family. Just because of the person that I am, I am a burden. I can't do anything to change that. You said it and you were right. I was trying to pretend that I wasn't a burden... that I wasn't me... but I can't pretend anymore. It's just a fact."

"Will," a single tear fell down Samantha's face. "Will, I was wrong."

"No you weren't," Will said blatantly.

At that, the car pulled into the parking garage and opened up the doors. Will sunk down in his seat because he heard voices in the garage. Samantha couldn't respond for fear that someone would learn whom she was talking to. She helped Will get onto the floor in the back seat and gave him the button that would open the doors. She whispered so quietly that there was barely sound coming out of her mouth, "Come meet me in the loading room once they all leave."

"Okay," Will mouthed as he laid down on the car floor.

Samantha started to turn around, but before she left, she gave Will a little smile. He smiled back, and he saw her start to cry as she walked away. He wasn't sure if she was crying because of him, or because she was going to get her daughter out, but he figured it was a bit of both.

He watched her walk away, straight into the building. Shortly after, she was followed by the three other people in the parking garage. Will assumed they were the guards. He made sure that they could not see him, but he kept track of everyone who entered so that he'd know when everyone had come out. After about fifteen minutes, it seemed as though everyone had made their way into the building. Will didn't want to take any chances, so he stayed on the floor and only looked up if he heard the door open.

It took a few hours for it to open the first time. Will stayed lying there thinking. He thought about where he was and how close he was to where he had been for so long. He thought about all the others who were still in there, and how Samantha was in there right now, explaining the new plan to Jaden and her daughter. He wondered what they would think of it.

After a few hours, the first person made her way out of the room. He watched a woman quickly move toward a car that was parked across the garage. She didn't see him, but he was able to cross her off his mental list. Eventually, two more people came out, got in their cars, and left the garage. He watched each of them leave and he was not spotted by a single one.

Finally, Samantha's car was the only one left in the lot. Will sat up in the back seat and pressed the button to open the doors. He slowly got out, making sure there was no one he was missing. He bounced down to the concrete floor of the garage, closed the door, and started making his way toward the building. It was crazy to him that he was willingly going back into this building, but he knew he wouldn't have to go into the room. Just the idea of being so close to it was hard on him, though. He wished they could unlock all the others and bring them all with them, but he knew why they were doing what they were. He kept reminding himself of the plan, so he didn't have to feel as badly about leaving them all here again.

Sometimes that helped, but mostly it didn't provide any comfort. Still, he knew he needed to do it.

He took hold of the door and pulled it open. It was heavier than he expected, so it was hard for him to open, but he was able to get it up and eventually and get in. He looked around and saw the inside of the building for the second time. The first was his escape, and now the second: Victoria's. After thinking back for a second, he remembered how to get to the loading room where Samantha had brought him just a few days ago. It felt like it had been years, though, somehow.

Once he got into the loading room, he waited. He wasn't sure how long it would be, but he hoped they'd be around soon. He didn't want to stay in here any longer than he had to partly because it was upsetting, but mostly because he didn't want to get caught. If he were caught without Samantha here, he wasn't sure what would happen. He kept thinking of this, which scared him immensely, so he figured it'd be best if he hid until they arrived.

He looked around quickly for a place to go and saw a cart that looked a lot like the one he had come out in, only smaller. It looked pretty old, so he wondered if it had been used years ago before the place got so crowded. Thinking about this one being in use gave him a pang of sadness in his heart for all of the others who had been in the room even years before he had gotten there. Quickly, though, he let that thought pass because he knew this wasn't the time for him to deal with it. Instead, he found a way to lift himself into the cart and hid himself away in one of the little compartments. That way, if something went wrong and there was a person, or people, around, they still wouldn't be able to find him.

Looking out of his little hole, he could see the very edge of the wall exactly where the door would hit if someone were to come in, so he laid there watching for that sign of Samantha and Victoria. He tried as hard as he could not to think about where he was, but his heart was racing with pain and memories from years and years of this torture.

While he was at Samantha's, he knew he was lucky to be out, but somehow, coming back made it all so much more real and the pain of it so much deeper. During his time here, blocking the pain and the horrifying reality of it all was the only way he could get through. But now being back, smelling the decay, seeing the grotesque walls and dilapidated carts that no one cared to deal with, and hearing ever so slightly the yells in the room brought his memories into the present. This time, though, Will could understand the full horror of it and blocking it out wasn't working. After a while of trying to think about something else, he finally caved and opened his mind the slightest bit to the pain he had felt. It was just enough that he could feel it, but continuously remind himself that he was doing something to fix it. All of the pain he felt all those years, and that he still felt now, would be what he channeled as he went forward in their plan. That feeling gave him the strength he knew he needed to be angry and passionate and persistent enough to make a change.

Will's thoughts were interrupted by the door swinging quickly open and then quickly shut again. He could hear Samantha's heavy breathing and Victoria's little "ah" sounds that he had barely noticed she made until hearing them again now.

"Will?" Samantha said looking around nervously.

"I'm here," Will said pulling himself out of the cart and back down to the floor.

Samantha jumped and started laughing, "Wow! I wasn't expecting that!"

They smiled at each other and laughed for a second in the same way they did the last time they were in this room. Then suddenly they both remembered the tension between them. The laughter faded and the smiles were taken down a notch. Will stared at Samantha with sad eyes for a second, wishing they could go back to that moment of joy again. Then his eyes fell quickly on Victoria. He bounced over to her and gave her a hug through the chair. She was unlocked, but still sitting there so that Samantha could easily bring both of them out. Will didn't let Samantha see, but a tear ran down his cheek. He was so glad to see Victoria again. As upsetting as this place was, it had been his home for so many years, and she was a reminder of the only good part of the majority of his life. Victoria kept her arms around Will, thinking a very similar thing. After a while, they let go and Will looked back to Samantha.

"You ready to get out of here?"

"Definitely."

Will started to pull Victoria off of the chair and she willingly got into his arms. It was interesting to him, because as he lifted her, her scent drifted into his nose and he paused for a second, startled. That was the same smell that he noticed when he went into the Keener house and when he stayed in her room and when he sat on their sofa. Somehow, even after all these years, the Servants couldn't take that away from her. Their family had the same smell, as most families do, and no matter the length or reason for the separation, there was still no doubt that Victoria belonged with the rest of the Keeners. Will smiled. He felt the small victory of the lasting link of togetherness that the family's smell carried, even when the Sovereignty fought so hard against it.

As he thought about this, he tried to keep moving. He carried her awkwardly around his shoulders and started trying to move forward.

"That's not gonna work," Samantha said laughing at them kindly.

"You're right," Will shook his head and sat Victoria down on the ground. She was laughing too.

"Let me take her," Samantha said reaching out, "and you push the chair."

"Okay. Sounds like a better idea," Will agreed and they switched places. Samantha lifted her daughter for the first time in what seemed like a lifetime. She wrapped her in her arms and held her close. Samantha didn't notice how heavy she was, because Victoria's weight felt right in the arms of her mother.

Will reached for Victoria's chair and started pushing it forward. It was lighter than he expected with the food and toilet boxes removed.

"Let's go!" Samantha whisper-yelled as soon as she saw he was ready. They quickly made their way to the door and got Victoria and the chair into the parking garage. All three of their hearts were beating faster than they ever had before. They were terrified that they would be seen. Samantha was basically kidnapping the two of them, or un-kidnapping them, maybe.

As they ran, Samantha talked softly to Victoria about how excited she was to have her home. Every few seconds, she would turn around to check on Will. She could barely see him over the chair he was pushing, but he saw her checking and would give a little head nod each time, indicating that he was good. He was so out of breath, however, that he couldn't call to her. He realized that he hadn't run anywhere since he was a kid, because in the room and in Samantha's house, he had no reason to and no room to even if he wanted. This was definitely the most exercise he had gotten since before the accident and he was definitely feeling the repercussions. By the time they reached the parking garage, he was so dizzy he could barely stay upright. He just followed behind Samantha as carefully as he could.

They reached her car and she set Victoria inside in the back seat. Then she came around to where Will was to help him with the chair. He was leaning up against the car catching his breath.

"You okay?" Samantha asked, realizing because of his past that that their escape must have been incredibly hard on him.

"Yeah," He panted. "Yeah... I'm good... Let's... let's just go."

"Okay," Samantha said and helped him get in the front seat of the car. Before getting in on the other side, she grabbed the chair and attempted to fit in in the back seat next to Victoria. It was a struggle to maneuver the chair and the car and herself, but eventually she got it in and was able to shut the door and get into her seat.

She pressed the button, and the car started driving home. Will had finally caught his breath and he looked at both of them excitedly. Samantha and Victoria both gave him excited looks back.

"We did it!" Samantha smiled.

"Twice!" Will reminded her. They all laughed.

As the car drove them home, Samantha went over the plan again with Victoria making sure that all three of them were on the same page. Everything needed to go exactly right or it wouldn't work, and they knew they would barely even get one shot at it, so it needed to go perfectly.

After about ten minutes, they arrived back at the Keener's house. The drive seemed to have gone faster than it did the first time. Will saw the sign with their name on it above the door. Suddenly his heart sped up again, this time though because he knew they were almost back to the house. Even despite all of the awkwardness between him and Samantha and Abagail right now, he saw this place, and it felt like home. He wanted nothing more than for them to feel like he was home here, too. He tried to remind himself of his childhood home, which looked very similar, of course, but for some reason, he could only picture the Keener's house. He wished he belonged here as much as he felt like he did in his heart.

The car pulled into the driveway, and Samantha and Will both got out. Jim and Abagail came running out of the house to help them unload as quickly and quietly as possible. Once they made sure there was no one around, Abagail and Will grabbed the chair, Samantha grabbed Victoria, and Jim went ahead to get the door for them all.

They pushed through the door as fast as they could and burst into the living room. Will slammed the door behind the family of four and leaned his back against it. They all started laughing. Abagail and Jim moved the chair to the side of the room and Samantha sat with Victoria on the couch.

It was weird for Will to see the chair, such a negative reminder of his past, sitting in the middle of this house, which was such a promising image of his future. It almost felt eerie that the two worlds could collide so much. He wanted to hide it somehow and pretend that that part of him had never happened.

He watched as Jim and Abagail rushed over to the couch to see Victoria for the first time in so many years. As soon as Abagail reached the couch, she grabbed Victoria, wrapped her in her arms, plopped down next to her, and held her. Will moved a bit closer and saw that she was crying. Her tears landed on top of Victoria's head, wetting her hair. Jim moved around them and laid one hand on each of his daughters. All five people in the house were crying now. Something about seeing this family finally complete reminded Will what all of this was for. Soon, if this worked, he would be reunited with his family, and hopefully every single one of the others would be, too.

But even more than that, it also really showed him what true love looked like. After years and years of each of these people fighting to see each other again, it finally happened. Samantha fought by trying to get a job in the room. Jim and Abagail fought by holding onto the memories and holding a place for Victoria in their hearts and lives. Victoria fought by holding on to hope, just like Will and all the others did. Will was slowly learning that love wasn't just something you say, it was something you do, and it could be a brief comment or a huge fight, but real love was fierce and bold and incredibly powerful, just like their love for each other.

Will moved closer again, not wanting to intrude on their family moment, but also wanting to welcome Victoria home. Samantha motioned him over, and for a moment, he felt like the awkwardness was gone. The hurt she caused was not, but he was able to look past it enough to enjoy this moment with them.

Suddenly, Victoria reached both of her arms out and leaned her whole body over toward the stairs.

"You want to go up to your room, don't you?" Abagail asked and Victoria smiled.

"Let's go!" Samantha said, and the five of them moved upstairs. This time, Jim carried his daughter, and she just as naturally fit into his arms.

When they reached her room, Will was filled with joy just by looking at the excitement and contentment in Victoria's eyes. It was like this part of her was missing all those years they were together in the room, and Will could finally know her now as she was able to be her full self. No one paid any attention to the part of her that the Sovereignty had so readily taken away from her. Today was just about her, her family, and the love that they could finally live into after years of fighting for it.

Chapter Thirteen

The Key to Forgiveness

The joy and love that Will saw on their faces was heartwarming, but it couldn't stop him from questioning his place in it all. Victoria fit back into the family so seamlessly and beautifully, but Will wondered if he ever could. Did Victoria fit just because she was blood related, or was it something more? And if it was something more, which it seemed to be, could Will bring that something more to their lives as well? Or, was Samantha right? He figured she was, but he kept trying to ignore it and focus on the present.

Victoria was sitting up on her bed with Abagail next to her and Jim and Samantha standing nearby. Will was standing with them and watching their joy.

"Victoria!" Abagail exclaimed.

"I missed you so much!" she said for the umpteenth time, tears still streaming down her cheek. "I love you so much!"

Victoria leaned her head on Abagail's shoulder and looked down at her lap. Jim sat down next to them on the bed and smiled, "I love you both so much! We're finally together again. It's perfect." That left Will and Samantha standing in the middle of the room.

"It is perfect!" Abagail smiled, looking at her sister and dad.

"Almost," Samantha whispered so that only Will could hear. She looked down at Will and shook her head with a sad look on her face.

"Let's go," she motioned for him to follow.

"We'll be right back," she told her family, although they barely noticed in all the excitement.

Will followed Samantha in silence as they made their way down the stairs. He wasn't exactly sure what was happening. His mind was racing by what Samantha could have meant by saying it was almost perfect. Would it be perfect without him? Or would it be perfect once they did what they were trying to do? He wasn't sure, and he didn't think he wanted to know.

"Come over here, Will," Samantha said as she sat down on the couch.

Will walked over hesitantly and sat down next to her, leaving an uncomfortable amount of space in between them. She gave him a quick smile and then started talking. He couldn't meet her eyes, so he looked at the mosaic painting behind her head. He still couldn't figure out what it was a picture of, but it was somehow soothing, with the colors mixing so well. It was soft and bold at the same time. He looked at it trying to understand as she talked to him.

"Will," she started, "I am so incredibly sorry for everything."

"It's fine," Will whispered, still unable to look at her.

"No, no, it's really not fine. It's anything but fine. I was wrong and I was mean, and you didn't deserve any of it."

"Really Samantha," he said with a bit more force this time. "It's fine. I really don't care."

"Well, I do," she told him. "I never should have said those things about you."

"You were right," Will said. "You should have said it, because it's true."

"But it's not, Will," she pushed. "It's really not true. Having you in our lives has been nothing but a positive thing, and it will continue to be if you chose to stay in our lives."

"Samantha, you shouldn't want me in your life," Will attempted to remind her. "I'm just going to make it worse. You're a good enough person for fighting for me this long, you don't need an even bigger burden."

"You are not a burden, Will."

"Yes I am. You said I am."

"I was wrong," Samantha admitted again. "Why can't you hear that?"

"Because it's not true."

Samantha stood up for a second and paced. Will didn't interrupt her, but he watched as she moved back and forth. She was clearly trying to collect herself and find the right words. Will wondered what was going to happen, but still, he stayed quiet. Eventually, she sat down again.

"Here's the deal, Will," Samantha explained. She looked deep into his eyes, and this time he let her. He could see the pain in her face and she could see the pain in his.

"My whole life is about love. I love loving people. I love loving my family. I love loving God. And when someone does something that isn't love, it hurts me. Knowing that my daughter and countless other people were being so completely unloved was about the most heartbreaking thing I could have imagined. That's why I fought so hard and loved so hard to get in there and that's why I'm fighting and loving so hard to get y'all out. But I'm also still learning how to love. To learn what love really is takes a lot of time. It's a crazy journey. It's a journey that I want to be on and that I am going to be on for my entire life. But that's just it: it's a journey. It isn't something that I have completely figured out yet. It's something I'm learning how to do each and every day, and I'm getting better at it, but I still mess it up sometimes."

Will was struck, because this was exactly what he had been thinking for the last few days. Love was something that he was learning, but he didn't know how to put that into words, and Samantha did so easily. Her words called out a truth in him, while her loved worked to call out truth to the world. The crazy part, though, was that out of everyone in the world, Samantha was the person that loved the best in Will's eyes, so to have her tell him that she was still learning almost made him laugh. She loved in a way with so much power but so much gentleness that it overwhelmed him, and he just wanted to one day be able to love partly as well as she could. Even just a bit of it would be an accomplishment. To hear that she felt like she was still learning it was absurd to him. She knew love better than anyone else. He let her continue, but he was incredibly shaken by what she was saying because it resonated so much with him and everything that had happened recently.

"When I was talking to Abagail last night, I was trying to love her well, but I was wrong. You see, I thought that loving her meant keeping her from pain. That makes sense, doesn't it? Because loving you and Victoria and Jaden and everyone else in that room means keeping you from pain, so I thought it'd be the same for her."

That struck Will too. It made a lot of sense, and definitely showed him quite clearly where she was coming from when she was talking to Abagail last night.

"I was hoping to keep her from the same pain that the Sovereignty caused you. I figured if I could do that for her, it would be the best way that I could go about loving her. But then I saw you standing there."

Will smiled at the awkwardness.

"And automatically I knew something went wrong. I didn't sleep at all the rest of the night thinking about it. During those first few seconds when I saw you, and when we followed you into Victoria's room, I was thinking about it a lot too. I originally assumed that loving Abagail meant keeping her from pain, but then 'loving' her ended up causing you pain. Love doesn't cause pain, so something was wrong."

She gave Will a look of deep thought and concern. Her words continued and her soft tone and vulnerability made Will feel comfortable enough to look up at her as a friend again.

"So, at that point, I decided that loving someone the best I could would potentially end up meaning that I was not loving someone else. I knew I needed and wanted to love my daughter, so I guessed that sometimes loving her meant not loving someone else. That made enough sense that I tried to come to terms with it."

That seemed right to Will too. By loving each other, the Servants had discarded all of the people with imperfections so that they could love the other Servants better. That made sense. Servants loving servants meant not loving him and the others. Samantha loving her family meant not loving other families as much. It was logical enough.

"But then I realized that I was wrong in that, too," Samantha continued to Will's shock. "Love doesn't cause pain to the person you're loving, but it also doesn't cause pain to anyone else. Love means fighting for those whom you love. Love means giving your life to those around you. My daughter was ready to love you with her whole heart. Love doesn't cause pain, so because she loved you with her whole heart, the pain that people caused you would hurt her, but the love between you would bring healing to it. The love would go deeper than the pain and I didn't understand that."

This idea made sense too, but it was far more confusing for Will. He liked the sound of it, but he wasn't sure it was fully true.

"I love Victoria with all my heart, and, Will, I also love you with all my heart," Samantha smiled at him. "I know that the Sovereignty caused both of you so much pain, and I've taken that pain on in my heart too, but the love I have for you goes deeper than that. I feel it so deeply that I am able to feel your pain too on top of the love. Does that make sense?"

"Yeah," Will said, definitely stunned, but completely compelled by her understanding of love.

"So loving Abagail doesn't mean taking your pain away from her; it means leaning into that pain with her and having love reach deeper and hold us all together. I didn't realize that last night, but I do now."

Will nodded. He could see now where she was going and his heart pounded in his chest.

"So, Will, having Abagail and I feel your pain isn't a burden at all. It's a deep, powerful, connecting love, and that love is so intertwined in us that we feel for each other. Love isn't a burden; it lifts the burden. By loving you, we are lifting a burden. I should have realized that yesterday and been overjoyed to welcome even more love in our lives, but I was confused. I was fed the lie of the Sovereignty that other people's pain isn't ours to feel, when in reality we only feel true love when we choose to feel other people's pain. You are anything but a burden, Will, and I hope you forgive me for what I said, but more than that, I hope you can let go of what I said and not feel the weight of it anymore."

Suddenly, Will really felt like he was able to let go of her words from last night. Listening to Samantha talk made him understand life so much more deeply, and the weight of feeling that he himself was a burden was taken away. It was taken away by love. By love that went deeper than the pain of it and connected him to Samantha and her family and reminded him that he was not a burden but another vessel for love.

"Will, I love you so much, and Abagail does too, and if you'd let us, we would love to love you forever."

"That would be wonderful," Will smiled up at her.

"Okay," she said reaching into her pocket. "Then I have something for you."

She pulled out a little box and handed it to him. It was bigger than a ring box but not by much. He opened it, feeling her eyes on him.

"It's a key?" he asked, pulling out a necklace with a small silver key on it.

"It's the key to our house," Samantha explained. "I want you to have it because I want you to know that you are always welcome in our lives. I told Abagail and Jim about it last night, and they want you to have it, too. You're one of us now, Will, whether you date Abagail or not," she smiled. "But personally, I hope you do."

Will smiled back and started crying. "I love you, Samantha," he said and leaned in to give her a hug. "I love you so much. And I love your family. I'm honored to be one of you."

They stayed there for a few minutes crying and giving each other a hug, and then they slowly moved away.

"Thank you, Samantha," Will said, meaning something so much deeper.

"Thank you, Will, for showing me more of what it means to really love," Samantha said.

"Thank you for that too," Will said again.

"It really is a connection," Samantha smiled.

"It really is!" Will agreed.

Suddenly, they both heard a noise. They realized that Abagail was standing on the stairs right where Will was last night, "Did you give it to him yet?" She called down when she realized they saw her.

"Yep!" Samantha and Will both said, and Abagail, Victoria, and Jim came down the stairs. Abagail was carrying Victoria and when she reached them, she set her on the couch next to her mom.

"I love you, Will," she said, and gave him a hug, too.

"I love you too," Will said, and they gave each other a short kiss. Jim came in and hugged Will, too, saying the same thing, and then Will gave Victoria a hug and told her he loved her too.

After all these years, Will finally felt fully loved and accepted. He didn't even know how badly he needed it until now, but suddenly he felt a fullness that he had never truly understood before. He belonged to something and someone and they belonged to him. That was love, and he finally understood even just a bit more about what it meant.

All of them, again, were in tears. With the addition of Will into their family fully now and bringing Victoria home all in one day, it was enough to overflow the house with emotions. They all sat there in the living room talking and laughing and crying for what seemed like hours as if they had no care in the world except for each other, which at the moment, was true. Their joy was enough to last a lifetime and their love for each other definitely would.

It was only about three in the afternoon, but if felt like the day had gone on forever since none of them had slept much at all. It didn't seem to matter to them though. Samantha sat next to her daughters on the couch, one on each side, and they faced Will and Jim who were sitting in chairs across from them.

"Hey," Jim said at a pause in conversation at one point. "We're still gonna do this thing tonight, right?"

Everyone remembered the weight of the situation suddenly and froze. None of them really wanted to, deep in their hearts, because no one could know what was going to come out of it and if Will and Victoria would get to come back to the house. It scared them all now more than ever.

Will noticed that all eyes were on him. He realized that that was what it really came down to at this point. They were all going to help, but he was the one who had to make the choice. "Yeah," he said sounding more comfortable than he really was. "We have to."

"You're right," Abagail said. "But we've got this. It'll be okay."

"I hope so," Will breathed.

"It will," Samantha smiled. "I'll make sure it is. I'm not losing y'all again, I can promise you that much."

They took that comment to heart and hoped she could be as confident as she came off now when it really came time to do it. Whatever happened though, Will knew that he was loved deeply and completely for who he really was for the first time he could remember, and that was all that really mattered. He smiled at the wonderful family he had around him, and knew in his heart that love was stronger than the Sovereignty working against them.

Chapter Fourteen

Tell Them Why We're Worthy

A matter of minutes later, while the five of them were still joyfully sitting in the living room, the doorbell rang. Jim jumped up and rushed to get the door.

"Hello," Will heard Del's voice as the door swung open. They all responded with "hellos" and "how are yous." Del and Jim made their way over to everyone else in the living room and then suddenly they all paused.

Del's eyes met Victoria, who was sitting in between her mom and sister on the couch. Victoria moved her eyes away as fast as she could and, instead of the happy noises she had been making just moments before, she started making a noise that Will knew too well. It was a single note of the many screams that had echoed around the room for years. It sounded sharp, scared, and full of pain. Isolated from the other screams, it felt new somehow, though, or at least more real. Del looked away quickly, too, and Will saw him take a small step backwards.

"I'm sorry," he whispered, directed more to the world or God than to Victoria. "I'm so sorry."

They all quickly realized what was happening, and Samantha stood up and moved towards Del. Abagail wrapped her arm around her sister and whispered, "You're okay. He can't hurt you now. I promise. He won't hurt you now, and if he tries, I won't let him."

This seemed to calm Victoria a little bit, but she still reached for Abagail and held tightly onto her arm. Her whimpering quieted, but she was definitely still scared. She refused to meet his eyes, but instead leaned her head on her sister and looked down at her lap.

Samantha stood next to Del and walked with him over to the couch near where she had been sitting. Del squatted on the floor in front of Victoria and looked quickly at her legs then back up at her again. She leaned further into Abagail, trying to get as far away from Del as she could.

"Love," Samantha put her hand on Victoria's shoulder, "He's not going to hurt you again. He knows what he did now. You're going to be okay. He's going to help us. Remember what I told you earlier today?"

Victoria did, but it didn't make it any easier to face her abuser in person in her own home. She tried to remind herself that she was safe now, but it was so hard to believe that when she knew how badly this man had hurt her, and how badly he could do it again if he so desired.

"Victoria," Del said quietly, but in a way that made it known he viewed her as an equal now. "Victoria. I am so, so sorry I hurt you. I'm so sorry I was so terrible. I promise I won't ever hurt you again. I understand how incredibly wrong I was now. Your family explained it to me. I am so incredibly sorry. I wish I could do something to take it back, to make you feel better, but I know I can't and I will live with that for the rest of my life. I'm so sorry."

Victoria continued to hold onto Abagail as she wept, both out of fear and out of remembrance of the pain. She saw that Del was crying, too, and that made him seem a little less scary.

"I'm here to help you now," Del explained. "I'm going to help you get into where the broadcasts are filmed tonight so that Will can talk on it. I'm going to help you. I promise. I know it must be impossible for you to trust me, but I promise I'm here to help."

Victoria pulled her head up a little bit to look at him, still leaning on Abagail. Her eyes rested on Del's face, but she still refused to meet his eyes. She knew he was trying to help, and she knew that Will and her family were having to be incredibly brave to make this plan happen, so she tried to be brave, too. She breathed heavily and her heartbeat hastened, but she kept her eyes on his face.

"Thank you, Victoria," Del said, understanding. "Thank you for being so courageous to look at me. I'm so sorry I hurt you." He sat down, cross legged, on the floor, trying to show her that he was safe and that he planned to be there for her and her family. He wasn't going to get up and hurt someone and he wasn't going to get up and leave. That made Victoria feel a bit better, too. He still terrified her, but she was beginning to believe that he was really not going to cause her any more pain. Her breathing slowed a bit, but she still didn't trust him completely. How could she? He broke both of her legs and kicked her every time she was on the ground. She knew though, that for the plan to work, she had to trust him enough to get her and her family to the filming room, so she needed to be strong.

She looked up slowly and looked him in the eyes. She gave him and her mom and dad a brief smile and then leaned her head back on Abagail again. That was all the bravery she could muster up at the time, but it was enough to show them that she was in and that she trusted him enough to move forward with their plans.

"Thank you, Victoria," Del said, smiling back at her. "I'm so sorry."

Victoria gave a tiny smile again. Abagail gave her a little side hug and whispered, "It's gonna be okay. Thank you for being so strong."

"Yes," Jim agreed. "Thank you for being so strong, Love."

As time went on, Victoria was able to get more and more comfortable. She was definitely still hesitant around Del, but by the end of their conversation, she was able to sit up and look out at everyone around her. Soon the attention drifted off of her, too, because they needed to focus now on what the plan was for the rest of the night. It was getting closer to when they needed to leave, and they needed to make sure everyone knew exactly what to do.

They talked through what was going to happen: how they were going to get there, where they would hide until it was time, and what they each needed to do once they got in. Will had been hoping to do something like this for so long, but the idea that it was actually going to happen was almost hard to believe. When he looked around to Samantha, Abagail, Victoria, Del, and Jim, he knew it was going to be a reality, and he was thankful to have some of the best people in the Sovereignty to do it with him. He was amazed they had gotten it together so quickly, but he also had a deep confidence that this was going to work. He wasn't sure if it was just Samantha's confidence exuding and spilling out onto all of them, or if he really believed he could do it, but either way, her belief in him was all he needed to move forward.

"Will?," Jim asked, "Do you know what you're going to say once you get on the screen?"

Will paused. "Yeah," he said hesitantly. "I mean I haven't really thought about it, but I know what I'm feeling and what I know the Sovereignty needs to know."

"I think you should have something prepared," Jim suggested. "It's up to you, but once we get in there, who knows what's going to happen, so I just think it'd be better if you weren't having to make it up on the spot. You should be talking as much as you can on the screen up until something stops you, so make sure you have enough to say."

"You're right," Will said, "How long do we have? Do I have time to come up with something?"

"We have about half an hour before we have to leave," Del told him.

"Okay," Samantha said, "So what do we need the Sovereignty to know?"

She asked this to everyone in the room, and they all started brainstorming everything Will needed to convey to all the people watching.

"You need to tell them you're worthy, Will," Abagail said. "But more than that, you need to *show* them your worth."

"Abagail's right," Samantha agreed. "How can you do that?"

"Tell them why you're worthy," Abagail said matter-of-factly.

"And why is that?" Will asked laughing.

"Will! Because you're wonderful. Tell them about what you did for everyone in the room for all of those years. Tell them the way you figured out the needs of each person and the words you spoke over each of them every single day. Tell them what it was like in the room and tell them how you overcame that and fought for those around you. Tell them that everyone else in that room deserves the same chance."

"Yes!" Samantha said excitedly., "That's exactly what you need to tell them, Will. If they hear about how you did that, then they will think of you as a person and realize that everyone else in there is a person, too. That's your best bet."

"Okay," Will said. "Sounds like a plan! How long do you think I will have to talk?"

"No way of knowing," Del admitted, "I could hold the camera on you forever, but if something goes wrong or if someone stops us somehow, then you may only have a few minutes. Because there are people whose job it is to count everyone watching, I think that they will probably be the first to notice. I don't expect that they are going to be huge fans of ours when we do this, so if nothing else, expect them to try to override us and turn off the programing. I don't think they know how, because even I don't know how someone would do that, but it might be possible."

"Well, I'll tell the story quickly and then elaborate after so that no matter what they hear what happened in there," Will decided.

"Sounds like a plan," Jim said enthusiastically. "I think that's really going to change their minds."

"Me too," Samantha agreed. "Do you think you're ready to do it, Will?"

"I think so," Will's heart started beating faster. This was really happening. "Are y'all ready?"

"I think so," Abagail smiled.

They looked around all thinking through what their role would be and what they would need to do to make this work. They were silent for a while, trying to make sure they didn't forget anything.

"What do you think is going to happen in the end?" Will finally asked to no one in particular. He put into words what everyone was thinking.

"What do you mean?" Samantha asked just to clarify.

"I am going to go in there and talk on the screen and y'all are going to be getting us in and keeping Servant Deena back. But then once we're done, once we've accomplished that, what do you think is going to happen?"

"I have no idea," Del admitted.

"Well, there's only a few options," Samantha laid out. "Either someone stops us, or we just move on."

"Move on?" Will asked.

"I think we'll know more of what that will look like when it happens," Jim said.

"Okay, but what if someone stops us?" Will asked.

"Then we fight to keep you on camera as long as we can," Samantha explained. "If someone tries to stop us, it's our job to hold them off. Don't pay attention to us, Will, just keep talking. We'll give you as long as we can."

"Hopefully that won't happen, though," Del said. "Hopefully, you'll get to finish talking and it'll all be received well enough that no one will have a problem."

"Well, I think the problem is in taking over the screens, not in what we're trying to say," Abagail explained. "I mean people might not like what we're saying, but they will definitely have an issue with what we are doing, right?"

"Most likely," Jim agreed.

"Then we're gonna have to just keep going as long as we can," Samantha said again. "Don't stop unless you're forced to or you're finished, Will, okay? No matter what else is going on."

"Okay," Will said boldly, knowing that that was what he would need to do.

There was not much time left before they needed to leave, so they used it to brainstorm all of the things that could go wrong. They wanted to make sure that they had a plan for every possible outcome. If nothing else, they needed to be prepared to think on the spot, and this was helping them figure out how to do that. In their minds though, each of them knew that this was such a big deal that it probably wasn't going to go how they thought it would at all. That was terrifying, but they all knew they had to do it. It was, in fact, the only option. If they wanted to get everyone out of the room and integrated into the Sovereignty, they needed to do something bold.

Now all they could do was hope that this was bold enough.

Chapter Fifteen

Anticipation

"Get up, Will," Abagail's voice fell on Will's ears, but he barely heard her. "It's time." They had all been sitting there talking, but Will had gone silent without any of them noticing. He sank back into the chair he was sitting in, into his mind, and analyzed everything that was about to happen. His heart started beating faster and his breathing was labored. He heard Abagail and tried to shake himself out of it, but he couldn't. He just stared forward, terrified by what was about to happen.

"Will," Abagail said quietly. "Are you okay?"

He still didn't respond. He couldn't. He couldn't get enough air.

Samantha walked over to where he was in the chair and leaned down next to him. She put her hand on his shoulder and leaned into him so she was beside him, but not touching.

"It's going to be okay, Will," Samantha whispered so only he could hear.

"What... What if it's not," Will whispered back.

"It will be," Samantha assured him. "And if it's not, you still know you're loved, and you know that we're all fighting for you and that one day, it will be okay."

"Are you sure?" He couldn't help but doubting her.

"Of course," Samantha told him. "No matter what, you are loved. I love you so much and so does everyone else in this room, and in that room too. Regardless of what happens, eventually love is going to win this battle. It might be hard at first, but love always wins, Will, and love will win in your life. People will know you are worthy and that you deserve just as much as everyone else one day. It's going to be okay soon enough."

"Okay," was all Will was able to say.

"Will," Samantha continued. "I love you. I love you so much and no matter what happens that's not going to change, okay?"

"Okay," Will said more confidently.

"You are so loved, and you will always be so loved. Circumstances change, but love won't. You will always be loved."

"Thank you," Will's breathing stabilized. "I love you, too, Samantha. Thank you for everything."

"Oh," she said suddenly. "And remember to keep that key with you! I'm not sure what's going to happen, but when it's over, hopefully we will all come back here together, and *you* can open the door!"

"I can't wait," Will said, and that was true. Knowing that he'd be the one to open the door because he truly belonged here was enough to look forward to and it gave him the confidence to do whatever it took in between. He knew if he pictured coming back, opening the door, and having the rest of the family all come in with him then he could get through the broadcast. He was going to be okay. Samantha told him so, and if he wasn't, she reminded him that he was loved which was important, but also that he was loved by her, and that held him together. He remembered first meeting her and all of the crazy things the had happened since. She really loved him, she loved him enough to fight for him, and somehow that was going to have to be good enough for right now. And it was. He was ready.

He made his way to the door. Everyone else followed except for Del who was holding the door open. Before reaching it though, Will turned around.

"Wait," he said, stopping them all in their tracks. "Before we go, I just have to know, what in the world is that supposed to be a picture of?" He pointed up at the mosaic on the wall. Over the course of the last few days, he had spent hours looking at it and trying to figure it out, and finally he just needed to know.

"It's not supposed to be anything," Samantha laughed. "It says something."

Will looked at it again. Suddenly he started to see. He hadn't read anything in all the years that he was in the room, but he was a great reader in elementary school before the accident. Still, it took him awhile to figure out what it said. He would have never thought about it being a word, and wouldn't have recognized it after all these years, but now it was completely clear. He looked up at Samantha.

"Of course," he said laughing.

"Love," she said. And so did the mosaic. All of the little pieces of glass came together to spell that word, and Will laughed because it made so much sense. Samantha had taught him what love really was, and now she showed him, quite literally, how to notice it. He smiled at the rest of them. They all had too in their own ways. He was so thankful for this group of people and was incredibly glad that this was who he was going on this adventure with.

He looked up at it one last time and then turned to walk out the door. They made their way out while Del and Abagail stood watch, and Jim and Samantha helped Will and Victoria into the car. The two of them slunked down onto the floor so they would not be seen. They were going to ride as far as they could so that the potential of people seeing Will or Victoria was less likely. It would ruin the entire plan if they were caught now.

All six of them squeezed into the car and they rode to the very edge of the town. All they could see around them were trees. They got out of the car, got Victoria in her chair so it would be easier to push her, and started to make their way into the forest-like area that no one but Del had known existed before their conversation a few nights ago.

They all trudged through the forest for a long time. It was definitely the most walking that Will had done since before he was put in the room. A few times he got tripped up by all the leaves and rocks on the ground. It proved to be very challenging to get through this much dense forest with only the tiny bit of his legs. It was challenging to get Victoria through the woods too, though, and so eventually they had to switch up their plan. Del and Samantha carried her chair and Jim held her as they walked. That went much more smoothly and they were able to walk faster after figuring that out.

"You doing okay, Will?" Abagail asked, sticking by his side the whole time.

"Yep I got it," he laughed. "Just a little slow."

"Not any slower than the rest of us," Samantha bantered. It seemed like it was taking them forever to get to where they were trying to go. Will realized though, that he didn't even know exactly where they were trying to get to. Del and Jim were the only two who had been there before, and Will could tell that Jim was still a bit lost. There was no real pathway, just random gaps between the trees and tree roots.

The forest was beautiful, though, and the setting sun bounced off the trees in a way that made everything feel a bit more magical. As Del and Samantha adjusted the chair in their arms, Will took a second to look around. He had never been anywhere like this before. He wondered if that was just because he was in the room for so long or if most people in the Sovereignty never went places like this.

It was crazy for him to see all of these trees in the same place. Every yard in the Sovereignty had a tree in it that looked exactly like every other tree. These trees were somehow more beautiful just in the way they were so connected and how they seemed to differ so greatly from the rest of the Sovereignty. This area was just quieter, less lit, and a slightly more natural than anything Will had ever experienced. The dirt on the ground was still hard-packed so that it wouldn't get all over everything and make it dirty, but every so often it was wet from the leaves or the moisture in the air. Will felt one of the wettest patches he could find. He had never really felt mud before, and it was one of the weirdest feelings he could think of. The stickiness was so interesting to him, and as it dripped out of his hand he chuckled because it tickled so much. He quickly wiped off his hands and kept going so that he could keep up with everyone else. The other thing he noticed while he was walking was the smells of the trees. The single trees in people's yards never gave off a smell, but having all of these together made their presence known not only in a beautiful area but also in a beautiful scent. It was deep and soothing to Will; it reminded him of the Keeners' house, which was comforting as well.

"We're almost there," Del said excitedly after about twenty minutes.

"Finally," Jim laughed. "Felt shorter last time."

"Probably because there's so many of us now," Samantha was filled with joy being surrounded by her entire family. "And a lot more to carry." She referenced the chair she was holding and smiled at Victoria.

"True," Jim said, and smiled as well.

"So when we get up there, I'm going to have to go in and get the video started," Del explained. "So I'll help y'all find a place to hide until we're ready."

"How will we know when you're ready?" Will asked him.

"Just wait about ten minutes and then we should be a minute or two into the broadcast, so it'll be a perfect time for you to jump in."

"Sounds like a plan!" Abagail agreed.

It was terrifying and incredibly exciting that they were all so close to pulling this off. There was absolutely no turning back now. Will was wearing the necklace Samantha gave him with their key on it under his shirt. Every few minutes he would lift his hand up to grab it and hold it for a second to remind him how loved he was. He felt then that everything would be okay.

After a few more minutes of walking, they could see an area where there was no tree where one was supposed to be. To them it looked like there was a tree stump where some Servants would be adding a new tree soon. As they got closer, they all realized that it was, in fact, not an actual tree stump, but the disguised entrance to the building Del talked about. They wouldn't have figured it out had they not already known.

Del walked over to it and said, "So, every day, I meet Servant Deena here and she unlocks this door with a code that even I'm not allowed to know, and then she lets me climb down the ladder first and then she shuts the door, locks it, and comes down after me. I have no control over leaving the door open or not, so I hope Victoria will be able to figure it out."

"She will," Abagail and Samantha said at the same time. They laughed, but it was true. If anyone was going to get it, it would be Victoria.

"Okay," Del continued, "Now y'all are gonna have to hide. Servant Deena is going to be here any minute."

They walked into the trees, a few rows past the entrance. Although there was nothing larger than the tree trunks to hide behind, each of them hid behind their own tree. There, they were hidden well enough that Servant Deena wouldn't realize they were there. Samantha and Del set the chair down behind a tree, and Jim set Victoria in it.

"I'll see y'all soon," Del said. "You've got this. Just get in there, and I'll do everything I can to keep the camera on Will."

"Okay," Jim nodded as he got Victoria situated.

Del started to turn away, but before he could, Will called out to him.

"Thank you, Del," he said with a tear in his eye.

"Thank *you*, Will, for teaching me and for being so brave." He paused. "And for forgiving me." He was now tearing up too, but wiped his eyes, gave them all one last cheerful look, and went over to meet Servant Deena.

Will, Samantha, Jim, and Abagail crouched on the ground pressed up against the rough bark of the trees, waiting in silence for whatever would happen next.

Looking down the row, Will could see each of them hiding still and quietly. He gave them all a grin, and they smiled back. Attempting to pass the time, he started playing with a twig next to him. He pushed it into the dirt and tried to see if he could draw something in it. After scratching the surface, he was able to get some dirt up, but not enough to draw anything substantial. He was so focused on his thoughts, he barely realized what he was doing. He continuously repeated what he needed to say once he got on camera. Suddenly, he started feeling sick to his stomach. It wasn't clear to him if it was excitement or nerves, but he figured it was a mixture of both. He tried to ignore it the best he could, but after a while he realized that he was shaking as he sat. There was so much about to happen that, no matter what, everything was going to change for him. He wasn't sure what it would be like when it was over, and that was terrifying.

It felt like he had been sitting there forever, but he realized only a few minutes had passed. The minutes went by slowly, but the longer he sat there, the harder it was to breathe and the deeper the pit he felt in his stomach. He wondered if everyone else was as nervous as he was. He figured that was probably right, but definitely didn't want to make any noise to ask.

He looked up to see Samantha behind the tree next to him on one side, and Abagail on the other. Abagail was looking out at everyone else, but Samantha's eyes were on the ground. She seemed to be deep in thought, probably going over the plan in her head one more time, just as Will had been doing. She sat there, still, and Will just stared at her for a minute. If it wasn't for her, he would still be in that room. None of this would be happening at all if she hadn't taken a chance on him and if she hadn't cared enough about her daughter. That was beautiful to Will. He hoped that one day he would have the opportunity to repay her somehow, although she gave him his life back, so he wasn't sure if anything would ever compare.

He looked over, then, to Jim and Victoria on her other side. Jim kept his eyes glued to Victoria, clearly still overjoyed that she was here. Will wondered if he was nervous. He always seemed so calm, but Will knew he had to be feeling something intense in this moment. He also noticed Victoria seemed more on edge than usual. She was quietly tapping her fingers on the side of her chair and gently rocking. Will figured she was just as nervous as he was. If she couldn't unlock the door, the rest of the plan would fall apart. He knew she could do it. He wasn't worried about that at all.

Finally, Samantha looked up at Will and nodded. Will got up as quietly as possible, and everyone else quickly followed. Abagail met him at his tree and gave him a quick smile. He smiled back up at her and that gave him the peace he needed to continue. Samantha and Jim grabbed Victoria's chair, and Abagail walked over and picked Victoria up in her arms. They made their way as quietly as possible over to the fake tree stump that would lead them to the broadcast room. They stood over it for a second without moving and just stared. They all knew what they were about to do and the reality of the situation could not escape anyone any longer. It was time and they all knew just how dangerous and life-changing this decision would be. There was no turning around at this point. They were sure that Servants somewhere had figured out that their eyes weren't on their screen at home and now would already be searching for them. This was their only chance to make their move.

Jim and Samantha set the chair down next to the stump and Jim rested his hand on it. Samantha helped Abagail lean Victoria over the stump and gently set her on it in a position where she could work on the locks. Victoria sat there for a second with her eyes closed. She took a deep breath, opened her eyes, and reached out to start working on the locks. They were so intricately woven into the fake stump that they would not be noticed had they not been specifically looking for them.

She started tinkering with the lock as quietly as she could, moving things around, twisting and clicking pieces in different ways. It was interesting to watch the way her brain was so clearly working deeply on figuring these locks out. Will kept his eyes glued to her hands, watching how quickly and naturally she started cracking the codes.

It was mesmerizing to watch her work, and Will could tell everyone else was staring just as intently. He continued to watch her and think about what was about to happen. He could still feel his heart beating from excitement and nerves, and he did everything he could to keep his breathing still. He went over in his head - for probably the fifteenth time - exactly what he wanted to say when he got down into the room.

Suddenly, Victoria pulled back and there was a muffled pop. She had unlocked one of the locks. Will could see now that there were two left. It didn't take her long to start messing with the next one. Within a minute, she had two of the three locks in her hand. Chains made to look like vines hung off the sides of the fake stump. Victoria worked eagerly on the very last one and everyone looked around at each other with solemn faces, knowing it was almost time.

Will watched Victoria's hands disconnect the latch of the last lock and slowly pull it apart from the chain. She laid the chain over the side of the stump and held the three locks in her hand. She set them down gently on the ground beneath her and moved her head slowly up to meet the eyes of her mom. Samantha looked down at her with a smile.

"Good job," she mouthed. Abagail reached down and gently picked Victoria up and held her lovingly in her arms. Samantha moved toward the stump and put her hand on the knob sticking out that seemed to open door. Before she opened it, she made sure to meet eyes with Jim, Abagail, Victoria, and Will individually for a second.

She quickly pulled on the knob and it popped it open like the lid of a can. She held it open just enough that they could hear Servant Deena's voice as they did each day. It was strange to hear her voice in person, knowing that in a few seconds they would be overtaking her broadcast. To think that she had no idea about their plans.

"That's how they plan to add it to the Sovereignty," They listened to her speak for a second, "It will come as a huge help to all of us and will make a wonderful difference in the way we live. I'm sure they will do it in a way that will bring us even more perfection and unity," She stated in her powerful, condescending voice. They had no idea what she was talking about, and no one else watching would care in a moment's time.

"Let's go!" Samantha whispered excitedly. "And remember, I love y'all so much. Love is going to win!"

Will took those words in his heart and would hold onto them forever.

Chapter Sixteen

John 15:13

Samantha held the door slightly ajar and looked around at her family, Will included. As slowly and quietly as she could, she started to pull on the fake wooden branch that served as a handle. As the door slowly crept open, Will couldn't help but hold his breath. Fluorescent light from the room slowly started to spill out into the forest and they could start to make out where the ladder was. The door was attached at the hinges and lay diagonally. Samantha gently lowered it until it rested against the side of the fake tree trunk and the ground. The door was fully open. It was her turn to enter first.

Giving them one last look with a brief smile, she pulled her legs around and grabbed hold of the ladder underneath her. Clearly no one below had recognized their presence yet, but they would in a matter of seconds. Will watched as Samantha quietly lowered herself and Jim got quickly in place next to follow. Suddenly he heard a scream. It was happening. Everything started to move faster.

No longer was Samantha in Will's sight anymore, and soon neither was Jim. They both made their way quickly down the ladder once they knew that Servant Deena had seen them. Abagail, who still had hold of Victoria, got the two of them in position to move down too. Victoria grabbed the ladder and was able to lower herself well enough to someone standing below and Abagail followed quickly after her, pulling the chair down too.

Will was left as the last one standing above the room. His heart and mind raced. For less than a second the thought sprang into his head and he realized that he could, of course, just run now. He knew where his family was. He could let these people, who he had only really met a matter of days ago, get stuck in all of this and he could hide away with his family and be fine. But he didn't even look over his shoulder to see the possibility of running because no part of him would ever do that. These people were just as much his family as the people he envisioned sitting at home watching the broadcast. He knew where his family was, and they were right in front of him, with him, fighting for him. The thought left his head as quickly as it had entered, and within seconds of Abagail descending, he grabbed hold of the ladder and pulled himself down, too.

Before he got too far down the ladder he reached up and pulled the door shut behind him. If someone was coming to try to find them, that would make it much harder.

He ended up just kind of sliding down the ladder by his hands on the sides rather than trying to go rung by rung. Almost immediately, he hit the ground and turned to see what was already quickly going on in the room. Del's camera was turned to point directly at him. From where the ladder left off, there was already the green screen behind him that Servant Deena used every day in filming. He looked up to the camera and could see that the room itself was only about the size of a closet. There was not a lot of room for everyone else, but they were making it work. Jim had grabbed Victoria and set her so she was sitting in the corner watching everyone simultaneously. Abagail had brought the chair up against the wall, and the three of them had managed to take hold of the completely overwhelmed and shocked Servant Deena. As Will collected himself for a fraction of a second, Samantha, Abagail, and Jim situated Servant Deena in the chair. Samantha held her in place while Jim and Abagail quickly locked her arms and legs in the proper spots.

It was incredibly strange for Will, and Victoria for that matter, to see someone without an imperfection stuck in one of those chairs. What seemed like a normal day to day thing in both of their lives for years, now looked like a torture device when it was used on someone who was in power.

Servant Deena continued to scream, but Del gave Will a thumbs up to go ahead and start talking. He was somehow able to muffle out her voice and focus the audio and video only on Will. Will paused for a second and then started to talk.

"My name is Will Josephs. I was born just like all of you. When I was eight years old, an accident happened. It was an accident in the Sovereignty, but I'm sure none of you heard of it because they hide things like that from you. And that's exactly what they did. After my accident, they hid me from you. They tell you that it's because I have an imperfection, but I'm here today to show you that I am not imperfect at all. The Sovereignty is imperfect for hiding, torturing, and isolating all of us."

Will wished he knew what was happening outside these walls. He could hear himself talking and saw that all eyes in the room, including Servant Deena's, were on him, but he had no idea how the rest of the Sovereignty was taking it. He was sure they'd be surprised, but did they stop listening, or were they intrigued? It didn't really matter, because he knew that, either way, he must keep going. It was the only thing that might make a difference, so he continued. At this point, even Servant Deena had stopped yelling and was staring at him. She continued to struggle to get out of the seat, but it was doing her no good. He looked at her and knew where he needed to go with his speech next.

"Can you see what Servant Deena is sitting in now?" Del turned the camera quickly to pan over to where she was on the other side of the room. He focused it for a split second and then moved the focus directly back over to Will.

"I was locked in that for sixteen years of my life. There were one hundred and eight people in that room, and almost all of them have been locked in those since the day they were born. There are toddlers in these chairs and there are elderly people. Women and men. People that are very well possibly related to people around you or even to you yourself. Every day, we were given a food patty and a toilet box was inserted into our chair. That was the only thing that happened to each of us for years."

Samantha urged him on and he knew it was time to get to his part of the story. The idea of telling the whole world what he had done suddenly scared him, as if he had done something wrong for sneaking out of the chair all those nights, but he knew it was crazy to think like that. He continued.

"When I was put in there I knew there needed to be more than just that. I knew that these people were in fact people too, not creatures as you so apathetically call them. They are people and they need love just as much as each and every one of you. So that's what I tried to do. I tried to love them all. As I said, there were one hundred and eight, so it was a hard task, but I was able to figure it out. Each night, when the chairs lowered for us to go to bed, I was able to slip out because my legs allowed me, and I would make my way around to each and every one of the *people* surrounding me."

Thinking about this was making him incredibly emotional and he felt tears running down his cheeks, but he didn't have time to deal with it. He just kept going.

"When I had my accident, on my last day outside of the room, my mom told me something very special and very true, and each night while I was in there, I said it one hundred and eight times: one time to every person around me. Some of them would say it back, some of them would give me hugs, and some of them would fight me because they were never taught to enjoy interaction with other people. Still I would say these words to each of them, and each time, I meant every word that I said."

Will's tears were flowing heavily now. He thought about his mother watching this. He knew she must be and he pictured her in their living room seeing him for the first time in so many years. He wondered what she was thinking. Was she proud of him? But he didn't have time to think those things. He needed to press on. He caught the eyes of Victoria, Samantha, Jim, and Abagail quickly and that gave him enough strength to wipe his tears away and continue.

"Every night I told them this, just as my mother told me: Child, I love you. And God loves you. You were sent to this place because the Servants thought that you could not handle the real world. They thought you were too broken, too imperfect, to be with them and that this room would help you. But they were wrong. Friend, you are not helpless, you are not broken. The God that we follow does not make mistakes. You are perfect, just as perfect as all of the Servants, just as perfect as anyone else. You are strong, you are loved, and you are capable. You do not belong in this place. You belong in the Sovereignty. Never forget that. You can be independent. You can be powerful. You are. So, use that power to one day let the Sovereignty know that you are worthy. Get out. You can do it. You were made to show the Sovereignty what they were missing. Don't live your whole life in here. Get yourself out. Show them that you are worthy. Because you are worthy. Friend, they will see us again."

As he finished repeating the words that no doubt were etched into his memory and his heart at this point, he looked up at the family that he had standing around him now. He saw tears in all of their eyes. He could tell Victoria was crying because she had heard those night after night and hearing them again now brought a new power to them because that was exactly what they were doing. No longer were they just words of encouragement, now they were a prophecy of truth spoken over them that they were fulfilling in that very moment. Will met Abagail's eyes as well and saw that she was crying too. He knew her tears were because this was the first time she was hearing these words that so deeply impacted his life as well as her sister's life for so long. Jim and Samantha were crying for a similar reason as well. Will smiled through his tears at all of them and they smiled back.

"My mother was right," Will kept going, looking straight at the camera, "I'm standing here right now to tell you these things about each and every one of us in that room. We are worthy, just as worthy as each of you, and you are missing out on us if you stick us all in there."

Suddenly, Will saw Del's eyes get big and noticed him lean back a bit. The smiles on the faces of Samantha, Jim, Abagail, and Victoria faltered a bit and then eventually disappeared. Will heard a noise. He knew something was happening, but now more than ever he knew it was his job to continue talking as long as he could, just liked they talked about. He wasn't sure what was going to happen, or even what was happening right then, but he looked at the camera and allowed more words to flow even quicker now out of his mouth.

"A world without me is a world without one of God's creations. There are one hundred and eight parts of God's creation that you are missing. People are made in the image of God, you know that, that's what this whole Sovereignty is based upon, but if you take some people away, you don't get the full image of God. If there is a group of people missing, that part of God is no longer represented. If we want to see the full picture of who God is, we need everybody, regardless of if we think they're less than us or not."

People were making their way down the ladder. Will could feel them coming in behind him. They were getting closer and closer and Will could practically feel their eyes on him. There were three of them, he could tell and as they made their way closer, he tried to talk louder and faster so that he could get his point across before they reached him in this tiny room.

Abruptly, Will heard Jim's voice overcome everything happening in the room, even being louder than Will himself for a second, "She's over here!" He screamed.

Servant Deena yelled right after him, "Get me out of here!" It was a command more than a plea for help.

The three people behind Will froze. They looked at each other for a brief second and then took their attention off of Will and went straight towards Servant Deena in the chair. It was technically their job to protect Servant Deena, not the broadcast, so that was what they needed to do. Will would just have to be an afterthought because with Servant Deena locked up in the chair, they needed to focus on her. Will stopped for a second, startled by Jim and Servant Deena's yelling, but knew again, that he needed to continue.

"Can't you see," Will said, gesturing to himself, yet not even registering completely the words that were coming out of his mouth. "I am just as much a person, just as worthy, just as much in the image of God as you. So is everyone that you refer to as a 'creature'. They're people. *We're* people. You need to think of us that way. Otherwise, you're losing us. We are here for a reason just as much as you are and shoving us into a room and leaving us to die doesn't change that, it just leaves you missing out on all of us. We need your help to get us out of the mess that the Sovereignty put us in."

The three people, dressed in all black, made their way past Will. He saw that two of them were men and one of them was a woman. The bigger of the two men went straight over to the chair and started trying to rip off the locks around Servant Deena's arms and legs. She sat there fighting as hard as she could to get out herself, and yelling at him to get her freed, which only made it harder for him to try to get hold of the locks. By the time the other two people had gotten there, Jim, Samantha, and Abagail had made their way to try to block Servant Deena in. The smaller of the two men and the woman tried their best to push past the three of them, but they made a barricade around the chair. So much was going on, it took everything Will had to focus on speaking.

Suddenly, the woman reached out and grabbed Jim. She pushed him against the wall and his head hit so hard Will could hear it. Shivers moved quickly down his spine. At the same time, one of the men pushed Abagail to the ground and tried to move past Samantha. She was putting up a fight, but he eventually had his arms wrapped around her in a way where she couldn't move. Suddenly, they gave Will an idea.

"Look," he said and pointed at all that was happening. Del gave him a strange look, but then flipped the camera around just in time to see the man shove Samantha to the ground right on top of Abagail who was now bleeding from both of her knees. Jim was still violently pinned against the wall.

"*This*," Will said, and Del brought the camera back over so that all the viewers could see his face. "This is an imperfection. When you search my name on your screen, just like you would a family member or friend, all that comes up is the word 'imperfection.' I was erased from the system years ago. But you saw what's happening behind the camera right now. That is imperfect. That is violent. That is terrible. I am just another person like all of you. Putting us in that room, torturing us, leaving us to die, that is imperfect and that leads to Servants doing things like what these three people in black are doing to my friends--my family--here right now. That is incredibly imperfect. We are not."

Will let that sink in. Del gave him a brief smile to tell him that he was doing a good job and that that last point really added to his message. Will was glad he was making sense. He hoped the viewers understood him and, more than that, believed him. With everything going on here, it was hard for him to even form words, let alone try to find new ways of convincing people of his worth. All that was going on hopefully was evidence enough for how deeply imperfect the situation that the Sovereignty was inflicting was. That would show the viewers that they were living into this lie that the Sovereignty was feeding them.

As Will explained that, he watched a full fight going on right before his eyes. The people in black were continuously trying to push Samantha, Jim, and Abagail down to the floor. The three of them were putting up quite the protest and fighting back enough to bring two of the three people in black to the ground as well. The larger man was still attempting to release Servant Deena while she screamed and struggled in a way that Will has seen many times before while he was in the room. The man, however, had never seen anything like it before and was trying as hard as he could to set her free. Will watched as Jim freed himself from the grip of the woman and move quickly to behind the man working on the chair. Jim reached around the man's middle and pulled as hard as he could. The man was most definitely not expecting it, and he and Jim both fell quickly to the ground. Jim landed on his back but spun around fast enough to end up on top of the man who was lying, stunned, on the floor. He looked up at him and tried to fight, but Jim had a tight enough hold that he wasn't moving.

Samantha and Abagail tried to hold the other two people off and away from both Will and Servant Deena. They were both bleeding intensely at this point but neither of them seemed to notice. Will did, though, and he felt terrible. They were doing this for him and now they were hurt. He couldn't think about it for long because he had to continue talking. That was the point of all of this. He needed to say as much as he possibly could. He continued to describe what it was like in the room and how everyone else in there was just as needed in the world as all of the people watching. Words were coming out of his mouth, and they were making sense enough for the viewers most likely, but he was barely able to hear what he was saying anymore. His thoughts were being drowned out by the sounds of the people in black hitting and shoving Samantha, Jim, and Abagail. They fought back, but not nearly as violently.

Suddenly, the woman turned and looked directly at Victoria who was still sitting on the floor holding her hands over her ears but staring directly at everything going on.

"Oh, you better not!" Abagail yelled and ran to block her. She made it just in time and she threw her entire body at the woman, knocking her to the ground. "You don't even know what my sister had to experience at your hands in there!" Abagail continued."Every day she was hurt. Every day she was kicked--just like this." Abagail kicked the woman on the ground as hard as she could. Blood was dripping down her knee and side of her face, but all she could think about was getting revenge for her sister. Samantha saw that it had gone too far and stepped in to stop her daughter. As she made her way over, both of the men rushed after them and tried yet again to pin them to the wall.

Will looked at everything happening and all the blood that was on the ground and on each of them and he figured it was time to finish. They weren't going to last much longer, so he needed to make his point.

"Don't you understand?" Will said. "We are not imperfect. We are just as good as all of you. If you let them, Servants will grab me right now and take me back to that room and I will never be able to get out again. I will never get to participate in the world and join in this beautiful life with all of you. No one in that room ever will if someone doesn't do something. We need your help. Please. Fight for us. We are worthy. You can see that I am, but I'm telling you, so is everyone in that room, if you give them a chance. Hiding them away, calling them creatures, abusing them, depriving them of the opportunity for life and relationships--that's imperfect. They are not. Please do something. We need you."

As Will was saying this, the people in black were beating up Jim, Samantha, Abagail, and now Victoria relentlessly, and Will could tell they needed to stop or it was going to get even worse.

He was able to catch Jim's eye for a second and nodded to him as if to say, "let's go." Jim understood and passed it on quickly, somehow to his family. Del continued to hold the camera on Will for one last moment, and he said yet again how needed all of the people were and how much they needed help right now. As he was talking, he watched everyone attempting to make their way to the ladder.

Abagail ran to get Victoria, who was now bleeding from her nose and cheek. She scooped her up in her arms before being tripped by the smaller of the two men who was standing right in front of her. He towered over her and Victoria on the floor, but Abagail was able to keep hold of her sister and slide around him. The woman grabbed Jim's arm and tried to hold him back, but he twisted out of her grip and went completely against his character to shove her to the floor. He paused for a split second and then ran over to help Abagail get Victoria. Samantha was still fighting with the larger of the two men. He had her pinned against Servant Deena's chair and was hitting her repeatedly across the face. Will could barely look. His heart hurt so badly knowing that she was taking this beating to help him and everyone else in the room. All he could do was hope that it was worth it and that they would be saved.

The man continued to hit Samantha, and Jim and Abagail turned around to go and help.

"No," Samantha yelled, "get out of here. Now! Don't come back for me. Just run." Jim looked to Abagail. They locked eyes for a second and looked back at Samantha. They didn't want to go. As they stood there, she met their eyes between blows and they knew that they needed to keep moving or it would just get worse for all of them. They hesitated for a second longer, but then quickly turned and ran over to the ladder.

The man now had Samantha pinned up against the wall, with her blood all over her face and his hands. He wrapped his arms around her neck, but before he had hold of her completely, she yelled out to her family, Will included, "It's worth it," she yelled. "You're worth it. I love you!" The words pierced Will's heart, and he was sure they did in the same way to Jim, Abagail, and Victoria.

The man slammed his body up against hers on the wall and closed his hands hard around her throat. She put up a bit of a fight, trying to pull away. Will kept one eye on her and looked for a split second to see Abagail, Jim, and Victoria making their way up the ladder, but still looking back to Samantha and Will. Will knew he needed to get out soon too, but he needed to finish talking first. Del still had the camera on him, but even he was making his was to the ladder. Samantha's words echoed in his head and that's all he could think to say.

"I am worthy. We are worthy," he said, and looked Samantha directly in the eye. "I am loved." She was the reason he could say that. She was the reason he knew that now in his heart.

He looked straight past the camera at Samantha, the woman who had saved him from the room, given him hope for himself and everyone else in there, given him a family, and showed him the meaning of love. He looked her in the eye, and knew he couldn't do anything to help her now as he ran to the ladder. All three of the people in black were surrounding her now and Will could tell the man was completely cutting off her oxygen. She kept her eyes glued on her family though, and Will looked back with nothing but love and sadness. "I love you," he heard her words from seconds before over and over in his head. "It's worth it. You're worth it. I love you."

Will grabbed the first rung of the ladder but kept his eyes on Samantha. He watched as the man slammed her head repeatedly against the wall. It made a loud, dense noise every time her head hit. Will felt himself shaking, but he couldn't take his eyes off her: his friend, his mentor, his hope, his mother, his savior.

He watched for a last few seconds as the man jolted her back and forth. Her eyes stayed firmly fixed on her family on the ladder. She held them there and gave them everything she had left in her through her eyes. Will saw the love. He saw the hope and the comfort and the grace, but most of all he saw the love. And that was the last thing of Samantha he would see.

Suddenly there was a loud cracking noise, and he watched her eyes go blank and her head go limp and her body slide lifelessly down the wall onto the floor. All color was gone from her skin and her eyes laid there fixed ahead of her with none of the love that Will had felt only seconds before. She was gone and a part of him went with her. He stared at her dead body lying there on the floor and everything she had been to him suddenly felt further away. He didn't even have strength to cry. He just stared. She was broken. The one who told him so many times that he was not. She was dead. She was gone.

The people in black started running to the ladder, and Will knew they would just as easily kill him too. He had to go, but it took everything he had not to run to Samantha. He knew he couldn't do anything now, but he wanted to. That was all he wanted now. Not to be saved from the room, not to feel loved, just to get her back. But he knew she was gone. He turned to climb the ladder before they could reach him, but he met her empty eyes one last time. Her body had already turned cold and grey. He saw her eyes set in her head and wanted to see them filled with love one last time. Her last words echoed over him still, but her body lying there made them sound different somehow.

He looked down at her broken body. Samantha lay there still and dead. It wasn't Samantha anymore, though. Samantha wasn't this weak or lifeless. Just her body was. Will turned from it and tears finally streamed down his face. He had lost her and lost a part of himself as well. She was gone, and all he could hear as he climbed the ladder was her last words.

"It's worth it. You're worth it. I love you."

Chapter Seventeen

Relapse

Will followed Del up the ladder and out of the broadcast room. The only thing going through his mind was the image of Samantha's lifeless body and empty eyes. He could think of nothing else and he couldn't even bear to think of that. He climbed almost unconsciously up the ladder. They were still moving incredibly quickly trying to avoid being caught by the people chasing them. Will could see Abagail with Victoria being held close to her and they climbed together. Jim was helping out from behind them, making sure they stayed stable. They had all witnessed Samantha's death too, and Will could only imagine what they were feeling. Probably a loss and an emptiness similar to his own.

The world fell silent. The people in black were clearly making noise behind them, but the sound didn't penetrate Will's consciousness. Only Samantha's image did. An image of her when she first came into the room and he locked eyes with her for the first time. An image of her before they left the house, sitting on the couch telling him he was loved. An image of her with her body pinned against the wall saying, "You're worth it. I love you." An image of her beaten body lying lifeless on the floor. Nothing else seemed to matter anymore, but at the same time, she had died for the cause of proving their worth, so it mattered more than anything in the world.

Will felt the key that Samantha had given him bounce against his chest where it still hung on its chain. The idea of going back to their home without Samantha haunted him. Now he had absolutely no desire to open their door. He just wanted to be back to where they were when she had given it to him. He would give anything to be back there right now.

All he could do now was keep climbing the ladder and try to outrun the Servants. He kept his eyes glued on Del in front of him because if he didn't keep his eyes there, he would want to look back to Samantha. Del climbed quickly as Will rose closely behind him. The people in black were getting closer to them too; Will could feel their presence nearing his back. He barely noticed though because he was already moving as fast as he could.

As he moved up the ladder, he didn't notice what was going on above. He followed Del out of the trap door and as he stuck his head out, he felt someone's hands on him.

Suddenly, he was being lifted out of the hole where the ladder ended and being thrust onto the floor. He looked around and tried to find everyone else. It took him awhile to figure out what was actually going on. He looked to his left, and saw that Jim, Del, Abagail, and Victoria had also been thrown down and were now on the ground next to him. Their faces were covered in tears and blood. It was terrible. Will could smell all of the blood on them and their clothes. He hadn't even fought and there was blood all over his outfit as well.

He looked up as his eyes adjusted to the darkness of the night that now filled the forest. Once he was able to see clearly, he could make out the silhouettes of at least thirty or forty people standing around them. They were wearing the same dark outfits that the people inside had been wearing. Will was struck with the fact that all of these people were Servants and were dressing identical because it was their job to keep Servant Deena safe. Thinking about Samantha and the way that she so adamantly opposed the idea of being called a Servant made so much sense in this moment. Servants wouldn't have killed her. If they were really servants--by the actual definition of the word--they would be helping and loving and giving to others. These Servants were not only acting superior to him, but also to her and the rest of the family. They had been anything but servants when they took her life. But still, they call themselves Servants. Will vowed right then to, like Samantha, never be called a Servant if that was what being a servant meant.

Suddenly, Will felt something in the grass by his hand. Abagail was sitting next to him, thrown down by the Servants standing over them. She placed her hand by his leg for him. He took hold of it and saw her other hand linking her to Victoria, and then Jim, and then Del. They may not be winning this fight, but Samantha was right, love always wins, and the fact that they had each other, for this second, was going to have to be enough.

The Servants stared down at them. They were completely surrounded. Will wasn't sure if they were going to be taken away, hurt, or killed. He knew something bad was coming. The looks on all of the Servants' faces told him that. They peered down at them with hatred and anger. Will was struck with the difference between their eyes and Samantha's loving ones. Their eyes looked much more like the ones that still lay in Samantha's body on the floor. They are missing the life that she had so constantly exuded from herself. These Servants had empty eyes, too. Will hoped that his still shone of life and hope, although in this moment, he feared they had more a glaze of sorrow, fright, and loss.

Suddenly, one of the Servants moved in toward them. The other Servants closed his empty space in the circle, so there was no way that any of them could get out.

"What are we gonna do to them?" The one standing in the center asked the others with a deep, ugly laugh.

"Kill them," one said. "Just like we did the other one in there."

'Now there's no use in killing more Servants," the one in the middle said.

"She wasn't a Servant," Will whispered, but only loud enough for Abagail and himself to hear.

"But as for these creatures," the man continued, "We could do away with them. They're no good for anything but chaos anyway."

Many of the Servants chuckled at that and one of them gave Will a sharp kick in the side. It startled him, and it should have hurt a lot, yet in all that was going on, he barely noticed the pain.

Another Servant stepped into the center. "I have a better idea," she said. "Let's take the creatures back to the room. Didn't that one," she pointed at Will, "say that it was worse than death?"

"You're right," the man agreed. "That way they can die slower now that they don't have a person to give them food and water."

Will looked to Abagail and met her eye. They exchanged a quick look of sadness, but knew there was nothing much they could do at this point to stop what was happening. Will just hoped that it really was worth it and that something in the Sovereignty would change.

"What should we do with the rest of them, then?" the woman in the center asked.

"Let's just get them out of here. They have no business being here, anyway," the man said, and then leaned into Del, Abagail, and Jim's faces, one by one, violently grabbing them by the shirt and spitting as much as he could as he spoke, "But if you pull any other tricks, I can promise you, that you'll all end up just like that Servant in there," he said, gesturing toward the broadcast room.

Will whispered again, "She's not a servant." No one heard him, but he knew it was still important to have said.

"Now get the hell out of here, y'all!" The woman yelled as three of the Servants in the circle yanked Jim, Del, and Abagail off the ground. They pushed the three of them forcefully in the direction of the town. Del fell to his knees, and they all stumbled, but quickly pulled themselves up and ran off. Will caught each of them looking back for just a second at him and Victoria. Their eyes were filled with sorrow and love. Even in the split second that they turned back to look at them the Servants went to reach for them, so they knew they needed to run. Will met their eyes quickly and gave them a deep, sad look, but nodded slightly, showing it was okay for them to go. They nodded back, with sadness and love.

Will watched the three of them turn and run through the leaves and perfectly placed trees. He and Victoria were left alone. Will looked to her and saw her rocking back and forth with her hands over her ears and tears and blood streaming down her face.

"Let's put them back," the woman who was still standing close to them said with a voice that sounded disgusted by the idea that she even had to address their existence.

The rest of the Servants flooded in around them, and Will felt their hands on him yet again. He saw them lift Victoria violently off the ground. One of them threw her over their shoulder and started walking. Within seconds, Will was lifted and thrust the same way. He could feel the person's sharp shoulder jab into his stomach and their hands wrap around the little bit of leg that he had. His head fell toward the middle of the person's back and he could smell the sweat and blood on their clothes. He realized that this was the man who had killed Samantha. With everything in his being, Will wanted to fight him and kill him too, but he knew, that if Samantha were to advise him, she would say do anything but that. He knew that he was going back to the room, and there was at least a little chance of hope there. If he tried to hurt this man, then he would kill him just as unapologetically as he killed Samantha, or even maybe more if that was possible.

So instead of trying to fight, he focused on staying as still as he could. That was the only hope of staying alive and, maybe somehow making a difference, after he got back into the room. He barely held onto this hope, but every time he felt the key hit against his chest he was reminded of Samantha's hope and love and it was the only thing that kept him from hurting this man.

Eventually he was shoved into what he figured was the trunk of a car. He couldn't completely tell because it was so dark outside at this time and they had hold of him at such an awkward angle. Once they threw him down, he was able to feel around in the darkness, and then he knew that a trunk was what it was. As he reached out, he found that Victoria was next to him in the trunk, too. She was shaking uncontrollably and still rocking herself back and forth. As the sounds of the Servants got quieter, Will could hear her whimpering and crying softly. He sensed the tears rolling down her face.

As the car started to move, Will climbed around the trunk so that he was close enough to wrap his arm around her. He wanted to be there for her the way he was for so many years as he spoke his mother's words over her. Only, this time, he didn't have strength enough to whisper the words. He just sat there holding her, sobbing. He had never felt as broken as he did in this very moment. Yet, somehow, having Victoria there was comforting him.

He kept his arm wrapped around her the whole time they were in the car. As he felt the car come to a stop though, he moved back into the place that the man had left him, so that they didn't have any reason to be more angry with him.

The light flooded in as the Servant's opened the trunk and reached in to grab them out. Will said nothing and avoided meeting their eyes. He was flung, again, over the shoulder of someone, only this time it was a woman who he didn't recognize. He saw though, that the man who had killed Samantha had hold of Victoria now. Will's heart broke even more. He knew that she was thinking the same thing he had been because she stayed there hanging limply.

Will watched the floor moving quickly under him, felt the key beating against his chest as the shoulder of the woman dug into his stomach, and smelt her sweat. He knew exactly where they were. He recognized the floor of the parking garage from when he was there with Samantha to pick up Victoria. It felt like years ago, but he was stunned to realize it had only been that morning. He would give anything to be back there, right then, but he knew there was no bringing Samantha back. Tears streamed down his face again, and he just left them there, afraid to move and get the woman angrier at him.

He watched as they carried him through the hallway that he had been through with Samantha while making his escape only days before. He could see the floor and the different colored paint on the walls. He remembered her pushing him in the cart and the joyful moment they had shared once he had escaped.

Within a minute, Will heard the terrible clicking of the lock on the door to the room. He hadn't heard it since he had been in there, and hearing it now made him sick to his stomach. He did all he could not to throw up, because that would definitely anger them. The door made its loud opening noise and they started moving forward again.

Will was thrust violently onto the floor. His back and his head hit the ground loudly and abruptly and he felt pain surge through his back. Victoria landed, just as violently next to him with a thud. Her whimpering, rocking, and crying continued. Will's eyes were met with the incredibly harsh fluorescent lights of the room and he could hear all of the cries and moans of the people around him. The smell of the room immediately came back to him stronger and more disgusting than he remembered it. There was nothing good about being back here. They might be right, being here might be worse than death, especially without someone to bring food. Then he'd have to die while watching the death of everyone surrounding him. Tears fell down his face for the loss of Samantha and the loss of himself and the impending torture of him and all the people surrounding him.

Will got one last look at the few men and women who were dressed all in black, who had killed Samantha and, who brought them back here. They kicked both him and Victoria a few times violently, and then slammed the door loudly. Will could faintly make out laughter from behind the door and the disgusting sound of it did, in fact, make him sick to his stomach. He rolled over and threw up. His entire body was shaking and he didn't have the energy to move, so he just lay there, covered in tears and blood, wishing for anything that could possibly save him from all of this. Wishing for Samantha.

Flat on his back, he sobbed for her. She had saved him, but he couldn't save her. Her attempt to save him and every other person in this room was what had killed her. And now, when he needed saving once again, there was no one left to save him. He was so overwhelmed with grief and hurt from the day that there was no way that he could muster up the strength to save himself.

"Will." He heard a whisper, but let it go in one ear and out the other. He didn't have the emotional strength to reply. It continued, though.

"Will? Will? You K?" Will barely registered the voice. There were so many noises in the room that he had forgotten about, that one voice barely reached over them anyway.

Jaden persisted, though, from his chair getting louder and louder. "Will? What wrong? What happen? You K?"

Eventually, after a matter of hours of staring at the ceiling, Will was able to speak.

"No Jaden, I'm not okay. Samantha's gone."

"She gone?" Jaden asked, confused.

"Dead," Will clarified. "Samantha is dead. And she died trying to save us."

"Oh," Jaden said as if the wind had been knocked out of him. "Oh," he kept saying, and his tears started flowing too. "Samantha Keener," he whispered over and over, as if somehow saying it enough would bring her back or bring them to the moment when they learned her name. Of course, none of it would work, though. Samantha was gone, and they were stuck back in here with no one but each other. They were locked in these chairs and in this room with no hope that they would ever even get food again. Will couldn't care about any of that now though. All he could care about was one thing.

Samantha was gone.

Chapter Eighteen

Together

"Will. Up. Up." Jaden whispered. Will opened his eyes, not ready to be awake.

The missing "He here! He here!" that Jaden used to say was the elephant in the room, because they knew that no one was coming today. No one had been in there since they dropped Will and Victoria on the floor. From what they could tell, that was about four days ago. Since then, there had been no one to come bring food, water, or toilet changes. People were being starved, and no one could do anything about it. Will hadn't eaten since the last time he was at the Keener's house. His stomach made noises, as did everyone else's, but the wails and cries of the other people drowned out their stomachs.

The room smelled disgusting and the people were living in filth. They normally smelled bad, because they were never able to be cleaned. The chairs were all overflowing and everyone was sitting in their own waste because no one had come to empty the toilets. The waste was running down the chairs and onto the floor, because there was no place else for it to go. Will let Victoria sit in his chair because her chair was still out somewhere in the Sovereignty, since Servant Deena was still in it when they were taken back. He sat on the floor sometimes leaning up against the wall, sometimes up against Jaden's chair, and sometimes, but rarely, against Victoria's.

Will felt terrible. In the depths of his heart he believed that he was the reason for all of this pain. If he had just been content enough in the life that the Sovereignty gave him in this room, then he wouldn't have tried to get out with Samantha and none of this would have happened. None of these people around him would be starving, because there would still be someone filling their chairs. Samantha would still be alive, and Jaden and Victoria were still so deeply upset that he saw it on their faces every day. He was too, of course. It broke his heart more than anything in the Sovereignty or in the room ever had before. He was convinced that if he hadn't chosen to do this, that they would not be sitting there, waiting for their approaching death, right now, and that crushed him even more.

Had he chosen to just stay in the room, his life would have gone on in a disappointing, meaningless, and mundane kind of way, but at least everyone else's lives would have gone on. Now, they were just waiting to die. Will could tell that some of them, including himself, were getting significantly weaker already and that it would only be a matter of a few days' time before death became a reality. After watching Samantha die, he couldn't take any more right now; he had never felt pain this deep and the loss of her truly was a loss of a part of him. The part of him that believed in him.

Jaden tried to console everyone, including himself, but it never really worked. Will appreciated the attempt, but he wasn't sure if he would ever be the same. Samantha was gone and even though he had only known her for a few weeks, she had given him so much, and he had never felt so supported. She had fought for him, believed in him, embraced him, and taught him. She had loved him, and right now, he felt anything but love, sitting on the cold linoleum floor of this room with nothing to eat and nowhere that he belonged.

Over the last few days, Jaden had said everything that Will had taught him to say, but to Will it had lost all meaning. He had gotten out. He had shown them he was worthy. They didn't listen. They didn't listen and they killed Samantha.

What was the point of telling them?

Whatever the point was, Will barely remembered it. Now he wished with everything he had that he could take it back. He wished that Samantha had never been able to get in to see Victoria. He wished that she was still out there, with Abagail and Jim, trying to make that happen. He wished one day soon she would come in, following Del, and give him a little wink. Then he would know it would all be okay again. But it wasn't. It wouldn't be.

Will watched every day as Victoria sat in silence mourning the loss of her mother. She never unlocked the cuffs around her waist or feet anymore. This surprised Will at first, but it made sense. Nothing was the same now. She couldn't just go back to doing what she used to do, now that her mom was no longer out there trying to get to her. She had lost something huge too. They both had lost their hope. Will didn't know if they had lost their hope because of their circumstances, or if Samantha had taken their hope with her when she died. He figured it was something more similar to the latter.

Apart from being so incredibly devastated that Samantha was gone, and so incomparably disappointed that his plan had so completely failed, Will was simply terrified. He was scared that he was going to die and scared that everyone else was going to die. It was unnerving to think that he could be the first one to die or the last one to die. He didn't want to be either. There was an unspoken terror in the room too, because everyone seemed to know that there was nothing they could do about the fact that something was really wrong. Will could barely take it anymore. He was so scared about what was going to happen to all of them. He would have given anything to just disappear. There was so much pain in himself and everyone around him, emotionally and physically from lack of food. He wanted to hide but there was nowhere to go. Even if he wanted to go somewhere and there was a place, he definitely would not have been strong enough to get there. He could barely stand up and move around between Jaden and Victoria's chairs, let alone get around the room.

He was in a state of constant lightheadedness from the intense emotions and lack of food and water. Everyone else around him was feeling it too, he was sure. It hurt him to know that none of them had made the choice that he had made, but they were still dealing with the consequences. It broke him to know that there was nothing he could do to help. At least before, he was able to provide a bit of hope, but he didn't have any left to give. He didn't have anything left to give anyone. Even just responding to Jaden was an effort, both physically and emotionally.

Seeing Jaden trying to keep his faith and enthusiasm hurt Will, too. There was no way that Jaden could have that much energy when his body was being deprived of food and water. It was terrible to see him so weak when he was always the one to be filled with so much joy and strength.

Will wished for Samantha, and longed for freedom, sometimes even wishing for the liberation of their impending death. Jaden put his hand on Will's head, which was leaning against his legs. He held his hand there in a sort of solidarity, trying to make Will feel loved. He felt Jaden's presence, but was hurting so deeply that love wasn't even something he could feel at the moment. Victoria sat in the chair next to them and looked straight at the wall, just like Will was, with the same pain that he was feeling.

His thought drifted around to everything that had been happening and all the hurt he was feeling. Though there were many noises, smells, and sights to distract him, he barely even noticed anything going on in the room because he was so deep in thought. It didn't really feel like he was thinking, though. It just felt more like he was empty. Sometimes things were spinning in and out of his head so fast that he could barely keep track of the numerous emotions he was feeling. At the same time, often his mind was completely blank as if there was something missing, because there was: Samantha, and the outside world.

Sitting there immersed in everything he was thinking and feeling distracted him so much from the room around him that he barely noticed when the noises and movements of all the people around him grew louder and stronger all of a sudden.

"Will... Who here? Up. Up. Who here?" Jaden yelled and started tapping his hand on the top of Will's head. Will lifted his arm to push Jaden's hand to the side, but as he lifted his arm, he stopped in the middle of what he was doing because he saw what was going on.

The door was opening.

He was so lost in thought that he hadn't heard anything, but all of a sudden, he saw it fling open in a way that looked almost impossible for a door of its size. It hit against the wall and no one pushed it closed.

Will watched as what seemed like hundreds of people ran into the room. He was mutually terrified and excited. He wasn't sure who these people were, why they were here, or what they were going to do. Their ambiguity was a chilling reality. Will could only be scared to a point, however, because nothing could be worse than sitting here left to die.

Watching all of the people continue to run in was overwhelming. There had never been this many people in the room, let alone this many Servants. They were running in and grabbing all of the chairs, pushing them around and pulling on the chains. It was shocking to Will, and to everyone else in the room as well.

"Will!" One of them yelled and pointed at him sitting there under Jaden.

"Will! Will! Will!" More and more of the Servants stopped what they were doing and ran toward him. At first, Will couldn't tell if their yelling was excitement or anger. He started crouching back and pushing himself into Jaden as much as he could. He was unable to hide, and they quickly made their way over towards where he was sitting.

Suddenly, someone rushed in front of him. As everyone started running towards him, he noticed someone who had been standing with Victoria make their way to the front of the crowd.

"Abagail!" Will said and tears flowed down his face. He really never thought he would get to see her again. He was so happy, but suddenly that happiness went away and his heart fell. Samantha had died trying to help him. What if Abagail blamed it all on him, just as he did to himself? He definitely wouldn't blame her, but that would mean that she was never going to really love him again. He understood why that would be, but he would give anything if it weren't so.

"Don't touch him!" She yelled at everyone else, who was bending in around him. "Just let him be!"

Everyone quickly came to a stop. The hustle that was swirling around them turned silent except for the noises of the people still stuck in their chairs. Will looked at everyone around him. Their faces peered down and looked at him. He was scared that they looked with anger, but instead he quickly saw they stood around him with nothing other than amazement. They stared at him with big eyes and smiles. Nothing that they were doing seemed like it was going to hurt him.

Suddenly it clicked. They weren't here to hurt Will and everyone else in the room; they were here to help them. Something had happened while they were in here for these few days and he wasn't sure what it was, but the looks on their faces told him that they understood that he was a person and that everyone else in the room was a person, too.

"Will," Abagail said, tears flowing down her face as well. She wasn't angry at him. She was happy to see him again, "You're okay." She reached down and gave him a hug.

"Aren't you mad at me?" Will asked. He quickly noticed that Jim was standing there behind them, now holding Victoria in his arms.

"What?" Abagail asked. "Why would I be mad at you? I'm just so happy that you and Victoria are safe now!"

"Me too," Jim said, also crying. "We've been so worried about all of you. I'm sorry it's taken us so long to get here."

"But..." Will still couldn't believe it. He was sure if he ever saw them again they would all be so angry at him, because Samantha died trying to help him talk in front of the Sovereignty. He never expected this. It didn't seem like they were angry, but Will didn't understand.

"Samantha died, though," Will kept going, "She died so that I could finish my stupid speech. Why don't you hate me? I'm the reason she died. So that I could finish that stupid speech!"

"That's not true, Will," Jim assured him, and put his hand on Will's shoulder. "She died fighting for the people she loved. She died fighting for love. It breaks our hearts that we've lost her, but she made that choice and she would make it again a thousand times: for you, for Victoria, for everyone in here, and for anyone who wasn't being loved."

Abagail looked at Will knowingly. "John 15:13," she said. "Greater love has no one than this: to lay down their life for their friends."

As soon as Will heard that it made sense.

"My mother," Abagail continued, "Was the greatest example of love that this world has had in a long time, Will. And the scripture is right, that is the ultimate expression of love. It sucks that it has to be, but it definitely was, and she wouldn't have wanted it any other way. What happened early this week made a huge difference, and she was a casualty of that, but she was part of that change. Part of that love. That's how she would have wanted it."

They were crying at the loss of Samantha, but there was also a hope that Will could still see in their eyes. He wondered how it was still there without Samantha.

"What's going on?" he asked, looking at all the people standing there, seemingly waiting on them.

"Will," Jim explained, "Once the Servants let us go and grabbed you and Victoria, we ran straight back to the house, and there were people waiting outside. They had seen us when you had Del flip the camera and so they knew we were part of it all. People really heard you, Will. They listened, and they wanted to make a change."

"So many people," Abagail said looking around. "This isn't even it. Hundreds and hundreds of people want to help. They believed you, Will. They know you are all people and they wanted to be *actual* Servants and care about everyone around them, everyone including all of you."

"So, what's happening?" Will asked, still a bit confused.

"All these people and more have been fighting this whole week to get in here," Jim told him. "They knew y'all needed to be freed from this room."

"We wanted to go about it the right way, so everyone pushed to get it actually approved by Servant Deena," Abagail explained.

"Wait, so she's okay with this?" Will asked, shocked.

"It took a lot of explaining," Abagail said.

"And a huge change of heart," Jim added quickly.

"But yes," Abagail smiled. "She wants to free all of you."

Jim explained even further, "She felt the same way that everyone else did. They were told from the time they were born that y'all were "creatures." They didn't realize they were being completely lied to. Once she realized that you were for real and dropped her initial anger about being stuck in the chair, she understood where we were coming from, and she actually wants to help."

"That's unbelievable," Will said. "So all these people are actually allowed to be here? To take us out?"

"Yes," Abagail said with a huge smile and more tears falling.

Will started crying, too. It had worked. It had actually *worked*! Samantha's death wasn't for nothing. No one here was going to die of starvation. Everyone was going to get out. He was going to get out!

"We did it," he said in shock, more as a question than anything else.

"We did it!" Jim said.

"We did it!" Jaden cut in with just as much enthusiasm.

Will introduced Abagail and Jim to Jaden. It was incredible for Will to have these two worlds collide. The people who loved him outside of this room, and the one who loved him so well while he was in here. It was beautiful to see how much love they already had for each other. Jaden knew that if they were related to Samantha, then they must be friends of his, and Abagail and Jim had heard all of the stories of the amazing things Jaden had been doing in here while Will was on the outside. Victoria was clearly excited that her family was meeting one of her best friends as well. It was about time.

Will noticed, as their conversation came to an end, that more and more chairs were getting either unlocked or pushed out of the room. He saw people carrying people out and trying to engage with all of the people Will had worked with for so many years. Some of them were hesitant to be around this many people for the first time, but Will was glad to know that many of them were only receptive to it because of the work he had put in. He had actually been doing something worthwhile all these years. His mom was right. They showed their worth to the Sovereignty, and they got out. Today was the day that Will had been hoping for every time he said, "Friend, they will see us again."

Today, they would be seen.

Today they were already being seen.

Will thought about all the time he had spent in here and all the years that shaped him into who he was right now. He thought about all the things that he would get to do now that he was about to leave. He remembered every day speaking his mother's words over everyone around him.

Suddenly he realized something. "What about my mom?" He whispered so they barely even heard him. "Is she here?" he asked louder. His eyes darted frantically around the room in search of her. The hope that was so depleted only moments ago rose up in his chest and he was ready to feel it all again after hearing that what he had done had actually worked. Now there was hope. Hope for a future. Hope for a family. Hope for a life.

"Over there," Abagail whispered and pointed towards the door. A woman with curly black hair leaned against the wall right near the open door; she seemed to be taking it all in.

"Oh..." Will didn't know what to say, but he started crying again, "Oh my..."

"Go!" Jaden said. "Go Will! Go to your mom!"

Will looked at him with the biggest smile on both of their faces. Then he looked at Abagail.

"Come with me," he said.

"Are you sure?" she asked. "I don't want to intrude."

"No," Will assured her, "I want you there. I want her to get to see who I am now, and you, all of you, are part of that."

"Okay," she said and took his hand. They made their way over to her. It felt like it took forever because Will had been picturing this day for so long.

Will quickly met her eyes from across the room and she started racing towards them, too. Tears streamed down her face. She was older than Will remembered, of course, with more wrinkles, but she was still his mom, and all he wanted right now was to be wrapped in her arms.

He let go of Abagail's hand and ran the last few feet to her. They hugged, and tears streamed down both of their faces. Will was struck instantly with her smell. It reminded him of when he was a child. It reminded him of her. He stayed wrapped in her arms for as long as he could, and she held him, as if she never wanted to let go of him again.

"Mom," he whispered.

"Will," she said.

They just kept repeating that as if it was the only right thing to say. She was his mom and he was her son and all was finally right between them because they were together.

"Mom," he said again. He looked up at her, "Mom," then he looked around the room and saw everything that had been his life since he last saw her. The chairs, the fluorescent lights, the linoleum floor, the white walls, the people around him: Jaden, Victoria, Jim, Abagail.

"Mom," Will said looking her straight in the eye and taking Abagail's hand back in his again while holding his mom's in the other.

"Mom, this is me," he said with tears. "All of this. This was my life. This is my life."

He looked back at everyone standing there behind him with big smiles on their faces. There was nothing but love between all of them, and somehow, that brought Samantha back in even the smallest of ways.

Will looked at his mom, speechless, wanting to say so much. He wanted to tell her everything that had happened. He wanted her to know it all, so he started with what was right next to him, because that seemed like the only logical place to begin. He looked up in his mother's loving eyes and he knew that she wanted to hear it all, too, so he started to tell the story, his story, to his mom, beginning with what was right there.

"Mom," he smiled. "I want you to meet Abagail, my girlfriend."

Acknowledgments

This book absolutely could not have come together if it were not for some truly wonderful people in my life. First and foremost, I would like to thank the people who put their time and talent into making *Imperfections* what it is. Thank you to Erika Thornes for creating the beautiful cover and adding all of the little details I hoped for. Thank you to my father, Dan Tricarico, for being the first to read and edit the whole book and for supporting the writing process from the very beginning. Thank you to Kim Cruise, for also editing it in its entirety and for naming a chapter.

Next, a huge thank you to two wonderful professors who have changed my life. First, thank you to Heather Ross for editing the entire book, naming a chapter, providing a blurb, and writing the back cover summary. Thank you, Heather, for teaching me what love and justice look like, and for our wonderful conversations that inspired many of the themes in this book. Also, thank you to Melissa Tucker, my professor/pastor/friend, who read and blurbed the book as well. Thank you, Mel, for recognizing Imago Dei in each and every person from the moment you meet them and inspiring me to do the same. Thank you both for teaching, mentoring, and loving me so well, and thank you for believing so deeply in the ideas of this book and for fighting for justice by my side.

Next, a huge thank you to Erica Kahn, Alissa Greenlaw, Kaelia Russell, Jessica Hong, Noelle Doctorian, Michaela Clark, Alexis Sagucio, Giuliana

Valia, Melanie Coffman, Cami Marble, Tori Berry, Evi Haux, Brooke Jones, Emilie Anderson, Ashlyn Craig, Anna Disser, Tessa Tricarico, and Claire Sunberg who read a chapter of *Imperfections* aloud to help me edit when I couldn't read on my own (and thanks for naming the chapter you edited). I want to take the opportunity to thank a few of these people individually as well. Thank you to Tessa for being my best friend, number one supporter, and midnight idea bouncer-offer. Thank you to Anna for listening to all of my disability-related rants that led to this story. Thank you to Ashlyn and Claire for listening to me tell the story of Will, Samantha, and everyone else for the first time ever, and crying, laughing, and cheering me on in that moment (aka those hours) and in every other moment that I've needed you to. Also, thank you to Cami for your constant support and love in this and all areas and for challenging me to keep advocating and finding creative solutions even when I'm tired.

Last but definitely not least, a huge thank you to my mom, Valerie Christian, for teaching me from the day that I was born that I am capable of anything and deserve to be included, known, and loved in the same way that everyone else is.

I am so incredibly grateful for each of these wonderful people and a few sentences will never be able to describe how much I love and cherish them all. Thank you all, and I love you from the bottom of my heart.

Made in the USA
Las Vegas, NV
18 November 2020